rené crevel

ARE YOU ALL CRAZY?

translated by
sue boswell

THIS IS A SNUGGLY BOOK

ISBN: 978-1-64525-121-7

FOR PAUL AND GALA ELUARD.

How hateful is life on earth.
A song by Fortugé.

ARE YOU ALL CRAZY?

RENÉ CREVEL (1900-1935) was born in Paris to a family of Parisian bourgeoisie. He joined the Dada movement in 1923, performing in Tristan Tzara's play *Le Coeur à Barb*e, before joining the Surrealists. In 1924, the same year that he was diagnosed with tuberculosis, he published his first novel *Détours*, which was followed by a series of other novels, including *Mon Corps et moi* (1925), *La Mort difficile* (1926), and *Êtes-vous fous?* (1929). He committed suicide in June, 1935.

SUE BOSWELL studied French Language and Literature at UCL and for a time taught French at Goldsmiths University of London. Later she became a translator for the Wiener Holocaust Library, and translated Arnaud Rykner's novel *Le Wagon* as *The Last Train* (Snuggly Books, 2020). Her other translations include Marcel Schwob's *The Assassins and other Stories*, Ilarie Voronca's *The Confession of a False Soul* and with her husband, Colin Boswell, Gustave Kahn's *The Mad King*, also for Snuggly Books.

ARE YOU ALL CRAZY?

I

The City.—Tattooed with an honesty flower.—
Her icy forehead smashes into a pane of glass.—
An alliance with the most equivocal of days, 31
October.—The man.—Because he no longer understands anything, about either things or people,
he rushes to see the teller of good fortune (as if there
were no ill fortune).—Mme de Rosalba, the clairvoyant, announces a forthcoming marriage.—Nine
months later the young woman, a redhead, will give
birth to a blue baby.—Death of the blue child.—
Birth of more multi-coloured babies, no less unvi-
able.—Here we make the acquaintance of Yolande,
a demi-mondaine, and some better-dressed wom-
en.—Mimi Patata, the star of the Folies-Bergère,
and her twin lovers.—The Prince of Wales and
his broderie anglaise.—Mme de Rosalba hardly
appreciates all these people and denounces the evils
of melancholia.—Imprecations.—Advice.—But
then who could turn the tide of destiny?—The rue
des Paupières-Rouges.—Long ago… at the time of
febrile February.—The mysterious flame-bird sud-

denly gushing from a slide trombone.—A crowd gathers in rue des Paupières-Rouges.—A speech by the City.—The man removes the flame-bird so that he can get some rest, on the highest floor of a skyscraper sanatorium.—The apiary full of sick people.—The gramophone hour.—In order to escape the shipwreck, the mountain dawn, his eyes fixed on the ironwork of the balcony.—Deprived of even that rescue, today in the rue des Paupières-Rouges, in the fog, the man becomes Mr Vagualame for real.—Yolande, all flesh and bone, with a very low neckline despite the cold, suddenly appears out of the fog.—Mimi Patata and the twins follow.— Yolande takes all these people home with her.

The City.

She's wearing a necklace of papier mâché faces, but her hair bun plays the part of the Arc de Triomphe.

This is how it was before the days of shaven necks, looking like the owner of a bistro, with her kiss curls, ringlets, fringes, waves, pigtails, the whole structure of hair and vanity complicated on the top of the head like an architectural fantasy.

Now the latest arrival from the Auvergne, leaning on the bar counter where her mop of hair is mirrored, puffed up with its frizzes, plastered with brilliantine, underpinned with combs and hairpins in scalloped style, a downmarket nymph, a female narcissus, but defying any vertigo—she gives you her word for it—for she has a good head, certainly, better than that of the whipper-snapper eternally crouching over a stream and naked, the strange-looking person, the spawn of a good-for-nothing, naked, outside, at break of day, looking at himself, go on then sissy, eyes, navel and the whole works, so much so that he finished up falling into the water, from where he was fished out dead, naked, more naked than the hand, since… but don't make me say something smutty, my good my dear, Auvergni, Auvergna…

…the ultimate slut anachronistically proud of the slimy and over-elaborate castle crowning her head, goddess of mayonnaise hiding nothing of what she knows of cosmogony, politics, local adulteries, whilst the oil of her sauce falls drop by drop into a bowl, is not the only one who inspires the City.

This large fossilised woman, moreover, always ready without being asked her opinion, to claim to be the epitome of taste, has remembered that Arabian ladies arrange their sequins as adornment.

So this daughter of the eldest daughter of the Church, on her asymmetrical bosom of which she has baptised one breast, the right one, *Sacré Coeur* (it should be noted, in parenthesis, that children of five years old find syllables at once differently precise and mysterious for the civil status of their toes), the other one *Panthéon* (*Pan* because this lady of doubtful virtue, a great fan of ancient history, does not dislike either a little flute tune, and greatly enjoys anything that makes a noise: slaps, rifle shots, games with machine guns, sounds of shooting and canon fire; *théon,* which can be explained simply as a mistake by the scribe who with the same number of letters, less pretentiousness and more plausibility could reasonably have inscribed it *téton*[1]), on a lower abdomen which has just enough of the obelisk about it to play at being a hermaphrodite and also has a composite name (three letters, each one at the top of a triangle in which lurks that part of a woman which is the most appreciated but the most vilified, then the noun *corde,* as if this flirty woman intended someone to hang themselves

---

1 Téton—breast; the three letters mentioned appear to refer to 'con', or 'pussy' which together with 'corde' gives 'Concorde'—the obelisk referred to then being that in the Place de la Concorde in Paris.

from hers), on her heart in the shape of the Palais-Royal, her navel which serves her as a bear pit, her arms, her legs scented with tar, she has imprinted the negative and icy tattoo of an honesty flower.

Honesty, dishonesty, small paper moons, sisters because of the drought of a greyness that they paint, if the sardine tin left behind at the pole by the explorer, careless of the landscape, has cheered the limping family of penguins, the man whom a pitiless iron hand, with no velvet gloves, has just snatched from the limitless shipwreck of sleep and sheets, his gaze bruised with the secret of his breast, a bleeding wound from the steel with which, after smashing his pane of glass, the city, helmeted and armour-plated with white frost, has just hit him, the man is nothing more than a moribund contour of the night.

His eyes? Stars switching off, two will o' the wisps back in the stable. With the clarity of his memories, acid scrapings of the sky and the debris of heavenly bodies, he tries nevertheless to put his face together again; his face continued along his neck; his neck… and so on, but the pieces of himself don't fit together well, don't seem to be made each for the others.

Of his flesh, of his wishes there remain only a few wisps of fog, stubs of a cricked neck. The woman of stone, the stony one, condescends to pity him.

"At daybreak, I dreamed of you and I wept…"

She dreamed, she wept.

Pity? What? A gaze cast too far away, the staging of the voice, and above all, these words of artfulness… Pity more hypocritical, more revolting than the League of Nations, the police, cauliflowers, braces, venereal diseases, glasspaper and sock suspenders.

The man lowers his eyelids, remembering certain months when the mornings smiled at him, with all the windows open, singing with a river's sweet voice, accompanied soundlessly by the shade's caresses. But suddenly autumn cracked with the salt of tears that part of the skin which cannot lie.

The man flees the bedroom of this miserable awakening and, in the street, he notes the alliance of the city and the day (15 October), the most equivocal amongst the thirty-one, of a family betwixt and between. Already it has seen even the fine insolence of the mimosa sellers grown pale. In order to better cock a snook at the puny bunches which these tinkers are trying to sell at the side of the metros, the aggressive nymphomaniac of vegetation twists around, and the gypsies no longer dare to move an eyelash when they have always claimed, quite rightly moreover, to understand the art of giving the glad eye in all its subtleties, and also with the nostrils, the mouth or the rings which they use for ear pendants. In their baskets, all the vegetation is weakening, liquefying, drowning the flowers, and the thousand pleats in their aprons are not too much to hide two lots of five fingers scented with the copper of large coins. It's the season of hands in overcoat pockets. No passer-by will save the smallest bouquet from the debacle, and the haughty travellers, who just the previous day were insolently drumming the heels of their clogs on the tarmac, blush at the filth which nevertheless easily covers the fine metal of their skin. Yesterday they were going around casting evil spells on people, their lips tinted fiery red to indicate to the big curlytops of the outskirts, always ready with their knives, that they're not afraid of red, but today, since only uselessly complicated skeletons remain of the leafy balloons of the chestnut trees, because this is the birth of death, these suddenly fearful creatures beg the cold, this freak, not to knife them between the shoulder blades.

With the light thrown upon this distress the man sees that he's never understood anything of things, nor of people.

He rushes to the teller of good fortune (as if there were no ill fortune).

Very quickly he climbs the five storeys.

He counts:

$$4 + 4 + 5 = 13$$
$$4 + 4 \times 5 = 40$$
$$4 + 4$$

But stop there! What if you had to subtract and divide, not add, or multiply? Beware of figures. Treacherous as revolvers. The magazine has been removed. They're taking aim for a joke. One bullet was left in the barrel. A diabolical, cabalistic, metaphysical bullet. Many adjectives are available to describe this murderous projectile. A nice little woman has nonetheless killed her nice little husband. Or vice versa. Talk about a misfortune! A model household, with savings. To think that the young woman will be twenty-one on Christmas day. Already a widow. So young. And pregnant. Here is a story worth repeating, all through the year, at mayonnaise eating time. It will give the City something to cry about, to dream about, to its heart's content. A good chance to change into something different, to float, an island on an ocean of tears. *Fluctuat nec mergitur*. It would be even better if the man was found, killed by the blows of figures, on the doormat of this clairvoyant who doesn't seem to hear. The woman from the Auvergne with the hairdo and the fossilised woman with the honesty flower tattoo must nevertheless never again be permitted to get involved with what doesn't concern them. So no touching of pistols nor of the numbers which go off on their own. Already this boy is not enjoying the air currents! He used to be made about the wind. A pretext for pretty symbols. But a city dweller scarcely has tempests available to him. In order to translate the hurricane, with medium terrestrial blows, he has left doors and windows banging. Causing a shuffling of the lungs. His body was never brilliant. Now he has a fever, he's coughing… He detests this rasping song, which, moreover, has finished by waking the fortune-teller, since some old shoes are dragging along at the other side of the door which is no longer slow to open.

The man gives a warning that he hates the past, and the present. He only came for the future. There is a void inside him. Of what he was, of what he is, all that survives is a frantic need to imagine. He closes his eyes so that no too-modern vision can come between the future and his palms.

She, the fortune-teller, can read the book of palms and destiny, she will read it and she knows her people through having seen so many of them, of all colours, some green and some unripe, since that time already so far away when, in the fairgrounds, under the name of Madame Rachel, a charlatan at the door of a caravan, she would fan out her tarot cards. A daughter of animal tamers, her eyes were never cold and she knows how to behave with savages and lovers. Moreover, she has always despised one and all, and now that she has renounced the turkey-red curtains, the eiderdowns inflated to ceiling height, of the travelling life, to become Madame de Rosalba, an armchair witch, the oracle of Les Batignolles, she harbours a retrospective scorn for the lions, those old-fashioned daubers with their pussy bow ties, who didn't even have the gumption to order a little ornament from Lautrec at the time he was at the Neu-

Neu amusement park painting large panels for La Goulue.

So, a first word of advice:

"If you buy paintings, young gentleman, since I see from this Ring of Venus, there, that you are artistic, don't trust the big bosses playing the bully. I knew one, I'm telling you, of those who wielded paintbrush and pencil. For proof, my niece had married an architect. He died in a heap of rubble. Shame. He would have built for you, not too expensively, the big house which you'll have a few years from now. And there'll be all the colours of the rainbow in the living room, and gilded wood! You'd think you were in the Palace of Fontainebleau. But that's for later, and now, now…"

With all her strength she tugs, she spreads out her fingers, so that her palm becomes an ocean, for the fortune-telling thirst of the former Rachel disdains glasses of water, even the one at the bottom of which Cagliostro saw Marie-Antoinette's severed head.

Madame de Rosalba plunges on.

A thousand leagues away, beneath the seas of the future, she sees: First, a marriage with a redhead. You will have been presented to your fiancée in a foreign country, during a voyage. But the wedding will take place in Paris. And what a wedding, with cars, fancy outfits and mass with the organ playing throughout. The bride wears the most beautiful white satin dress with a train. Her veil of Brussels lace is anything but trashy. There are many guests. And not just anybodies. The President of the Republic in person. If his wife hasn't come, no need to make a song and dance, it's just that he's a bachelor. The Pope has sent his blessing and the afternoon is spent in drinking champagne.

Honeymoon in Italy.

In Venice the redhead realises she's pregnant. Nine months later she gives birth to a blue baby. The nurse can't believe what she's seeing, but the doctor, another who likes painting and knows about it, thinks the mummy and baby would make a pretty water colour. Alas! This strange baby dies young, at the age of three minutes. Dear innocent, whose head was too heavy for your fragile neck, your poor mother over the coming years will give you a whole rainbow of brothers and sisters, no more viable than you. It's the fault of the daddy who has tired himself out too much. This is confirmed by his palms which are in turn furrowed and swollen by desires. The Mount of Venus, for example, is a real little Himalaya. But as for the reliefs, the peaks and chains themselves signify valleys, dips, hollows, depressions. There is certainly mist on the sides, from foot to peak, of the Mount of Love, that's why Monsieur has a melancholic soul.

The clairvoyant repeats these final syllables, rapidly enough for them to metamorphose into a single word with a cabalistic appeal.

Melancholic, melancholic, melancholic, now Madame de Rosalba is in a trance.

Melancholic, melancholic.

Thunder rolls.

Madame de Rosalba is not pleased.

Madame de Rosalba threatens, curses.

Melancholic, melancholic.

She'll give you any old rubbish, zig and zig, toc and toc. Monsieur enjoys his rumpy-pumpy. Monsieur puts his tongue into all mouths, without it even occurring to him that it's more indiscreet, more dangerous too, than reading correspondence that's not addressed to you.

Melancholic, melancholic.

Monsieur wants to know about the future: Well, he'll eat asparagus in the middle of winter, and caviar and oysters at every meal. He likes to lift his elbow. Watch out, then… From aperitifs to digestifs, he'll be in a fine state. In winter: Monte-Carlo. Trenteet-quarante, roulette, baccarat and the whole caboodle. Adventuresses walk along by the sea, beneath the palm trees, dressed to the nines. The redhead's dowry, certainly, will not last long. In the spring, return to Paris. Races at Auteuil and Longchamp. A light grey top hat, nose full of coke, a carnation in the buttonhole. You can lose all you wish, but the worst is an acquaintance, a Yolande, about whom Madame Rosalba is scarcely complimentary. Nevertheless, let us see a little of what happens at the home of this demi-mondaine, one of the best-dressed, a false pearl no doubt, but whose setting is not displeasing. The mistress of the house sits majestically in the cathedra she bought for its weight in gold, at the Sarah Bernhardt sale. Fine furnishings, historic. Yolande is full of herself, dominating the guests, who have only small Algerian carved wooden stools to sit on, inlaid with mother-of-pearl, a gift from the grandson of Abd el-Kader himself. On the floor there are only bear and leopard skins; on the walls, hangings, silk brocades, lacquer wares, pictures, damasks, velvets, and on the marble tables and gilded wooden consoles, Chinese vases with great bouquets of feathers, statuettes, snuff boxes, liqueur cabinets, every object a precious one and, for all tastes, from museum pieces to knick-knacks, to baubles, but all the height of luxury…

Madame de Rosalba despises the riches she's describing. With her constant contacts with the beyond, how could she allow herself to be moved by an earthly display, however splendid? So from the height of her dream state she sends down her indignant thunderbolts upon the scandalous Yolande and her salon, where, certainly, there are some highly placed people, but some highly placed people who would do better to go elsewhere, starting with the Prince of Wales, sitting on one of Abd el-Kader's grandson's twelve stools working away at his broderie anglaise, naturally.

His aide-de-camp is swigging champagne with Mimi Patata, the star of the Folies-Bergère, a former singer who has been seen dancing around since 1900 and who, for sure, is getting close to fifty, but she's on the ball, that big woman, she knows how to get a man to fit like a glove, and to get her fill of young flesh. For example: her two lovers, two young twins recently arrived from Sweden, two slim pink and blond boys, with eyes hollowed mauve by fraternal incest and the demands of the old warrior woman. They are standing one to the right and the other to the left of the heir to the English throne, and Yolande, watching this group, Yolande at the height of her glory, seated in her cathedra, feels an intoxication, the like of which during her long love life was equalled only by her joy, on the day, already years and years ago, when for her birthday she received some bronze mantelpiece garnitures, a statue clock and two candelabras, a gift from the first of her rich admirers, whom she did not delay in ruining for, as Madame de Rosalba insists, you cannot say that Yolande is the bee's knees.

A kept woman, that's all.

There are stories about her.

Her lovely manners? It's all put on.

I myself would smack her bottom, the stuck-up woman with her airs and graces like a queen descending from her throne. She's going to have a go at Patata. Let's listen. First, compliments on the twins. These two young things in a bed... ah... ah... But Yolande is slyness, cunning personified. She insinuates: "They look as if they're very fond of each other, perhaps a little too much, don't you find, dear Mimi, your Scandinavians?"

Mimi chokes on her words.

Yolande goes on questioning:

"Don't they speak a single language other than Swedish? They're very silent. In good health? For someone from a country which is said to do so much gymnastics they do seem a little like spun glass deer. Of course they feed on rice powder. One point and that's everything. Do they know how to dance? If so, Mimi, why not order a sketch? Good Lord, you have to refresh your image from time to time. And then you'd have a lovely poster. Each of them would be a Patatus."

Yolande, who every morning takes lessons in Latin and in fencing, knows that:

Patatus + Patatus = Patati.

They would announce Patati and Patata.

All Paris would come rushing…

Mimi, sensing that she's being made fun of, turns her back on the rude woman, goes to curtsy to the Prince of Wales and ask him what he thinks of her twins…

"*Twins,*" hisses Yolande. "I'll give you twins, with English sauce. Madame doesn't know how to spell but Madame thinks she's a mini Shakespeare. Do your curtsy. It's obvious you had your first lessons in behaviour in the infants' school in rue Mouffetard. Simper. Smile. Take advantage of what's left, for you won't be invited again with high-born people. Patata, old potato."

What a temper, what vulgarity!

Madame de Rosalba is shocked.

And then, with these women of loose morals one never knows what to think. Not five minutes ago Yolande was enjoying her triumph and here she is close to getting angry, to using coarse language. She's getting on her high horse, but it's not her father, a cab driver, who gave her lessons in fashionable horsemanship. There's no point in her sleeping in a bed that, they say, belonged to the Empress of China, sitting in Sarah Bernhardt's authentic cathedra and eating at a table which, long ago, belonged to Madame de Poincaré, the furniture of these great ladies has not left its mark on her any more, besides, in reality than figuratively, since she continues to paint her face and body with white liquid powder make-up when fashion has led other women to walnut colour.

Rather than coming, with his embroidery, to the home of a loose woman the son of the King of England would have been better marrying a Belgian or Italian princess, as his family wished him to. And, in the paradise of sensible hearts, what must the late good Queen Victoria be thinking, she, finally, who did not have melancholia. Her solid qualities did have their reward, both in the British Isles and in the Dominions, just as, according to the same and just principal, the cowardice of the current heir is punished. Already he is suffering. Yolande's attitude and words hurt his fragile and delicate nature. And then the twins, simply through their professional training, start to make eyes at him. Shyly, he blushes, and to make a better show he suggests a black mass, to which the orchestra's black musicians, playing quietly in a corner, will make their contribution.

Now Madame de Rosalba, who doesn't want to sink into the ocean of ignominy, makes a move, resurfaces, upset but inexorable, and comes out of the trance which had immersed her in the other side.

To the man who must be present at the sacrilege to which the dark chocolate musicians will be the negative hosts, to the man with fog in his heart, to Mr Melancholia, she gives maternal and strict advice:

"Deep down, you don't know what to do, my boy. That's the bottom of it. Let the Prince of Wales be an example to you. At least he has a saving grace: his broderie anglaise. But you! You think, you meditate? Humbug. If you want people to laugh at you, put a notice on your door:

"The Thinker's House

"There are butchers, bakeries, charcuteries, groceries, breweries. There are no thinkeries. Lazy man. Are you going to tell me that fate is ordained, up in the stars, way beyond the Rosalba woman's fifth floor? Fair enough, I'm just dust. Is that any reason why you should play at being a nonentity from one end of the year to the other? Make a bit of an effort, for goodness' sake. What if you took, for example, the sabre of your great-grandfather, who was a brave moustachioed colonel? Look at the map of the world. It is stuffed with peoples waiting under palm trees, on islands, behind dunes, for someone to come and smash in their heads. Remember how you used to love singing 'Fanfan la Tulipe'[1], at the time of the whitewashed images. At that time you were a perfect little angel, with the scent of the good earth of France. At night, in your neat little

1 A *chanson* written in 1819 by Émile Debraux which later inspired a number of plays, operettas and films.

bed you would have a nice dream that you had cut off the ears of the King of Dahomey. Your mother would season them with vinegar for all the family to enjoy. A lovely child, you were completely unselfish. Today, you think only of yourself. You detest your past like an elder brother. You love only that great whore of a town which takes away your youth and health. It's not even four o'clock yet and already you're dreaming of your midnight encounters. A green monkey would blush with all that. You, you're not even ashamed."

And Madame Rosalba's indignation continues.

Melancholic, melancholic, melancholic.

She falls into a trance.

She sees a small dainty mother, penniless because of you, dining on soused herring in her kitchen, whilst looking at the Tour St-Jacques.

The dainty little mother has just received a letter in which the anonymous author writes that her son frequents strange pougnacish[1] women. The dainty mother is not used to such a writing style. She tries to imagine the ladies

---

1 In French, 'pougnaquées', an invented word, a combination of 'pugnacité' (pugnacity) and 'gnaque', 'combativity'.

in question (it's Yolande and Mimi who are referred to, of course). She looks for the word *pougnacish* in the big seven-volume Larousse dictionary, the only one saved from a library and sold by a court order. She is getting irritated. She can't find it. Now she's sobbing, for this unworthy son, if he continues on this path, will see his spinal column emptied of its marrow. The tide of destiny could not be turned by advice, however rational. No doubt the best thing would be to have a good soup of water lilies every evening before going to bed. The children of chaste Switzerland, for example, during the time of their military service, would happily swallow several bowlfuls of this broth daily. Thus they returned as virgins to their mountains, ready to make children who would be neither blue nor mauve...

But he just smiles. He doesn't care. He sticks to his melancholia. Madame de Rosalba therefore has nothing further but to give a little list of catastrophes:

Divorce.

A dreadful scandal of public morality.

Prison.

Railway accidents.

A foul disease.

Ruin.

Dishonour.

Paralysis around the age of forty. Thirty years in a wheelchair. Then death. With the water lily soup these misfortunes could have been avoided. You would have become a centenarian. But let's say no more. Madame de Rosalba has nothing more to add. That will be twenty francs.

Mr Melancholia is already on his way downstairs.

Taking pity on him, Madame de Rosalba calls to him over the bannisters that she knows a recipe which might bring him happiness. Not for chastity this time, but on the contrary, for seduction, since he's bent on—at his own risk and peril—trying to play the Don Juan.

500 grams of rhubarb.

1 litre of white wine.

Leave the rhubarb to macerate for 24 hours in the white wine. Then wash your hair with this mixture. Rinse well with water. This will give you the most splendid blondness certain to have an effect on older people for, since it's a question of love, one more piece of advice: never go for the youngsters. Do not run after those silly girls who lead on those who pursue them and finally give themselves spontaneously to those who look as if they're going to leave them for more mature beauties. Thus the redhead, if she's going to offer her freckled hand, it will be because her mother, yet another character that one, said something in passing, allowed a glimpse of her soft spot for the future. To sum up then: rhubarb, white wine. Smiles for the fifty-year-olds. As for the blue baby, baptise him as soon as he's born, so that the little angel can go directly to heaven. Goodbye and thank you.

The man leaves the clairvoyant's house.

The City, again, hisses to him with icy pity: "I dreamed of you and I wept."

A single sentence. That's all she finds to say, the great fossil. But, as in the song, here comes the autumn wind. Like an evil shepherd, he drives his flock, the clouds, and their shadows, falling from the sky to the earth, multiply, deformed like moving monsters, even faster than threatening, whose madness, suddenly, sweeps, darkens the water of too bright regards.

The man scoffs:

"Now then, City, you who claimed in your pride to invent the most scandalous secrets, you have the audacity, that gentle masterpiece, to shiver all over. You're hysterical! You're fit for La Salpêtrière[1]. Saltpetre is the syphilis of walls. You've already lost your hair. Your pebbly skin is covered with scabs of plaster. Your dear skull is hurting below its tarmacadam. Your limbs are twisted. Take note. I once knew, in a village, a woman, no doubt already too old for what is called premature dementia but who nevertheless thought she was a corkscrew, so much so that she ended by becoming one. When she died it was impossible to straighten her out, despite them pulling on her head, her hands, her feet. As for getting her into a coffin when she was so twisted, you might as well hope to make the Madeleine's steps out of a spiral staircase. So instead of a coffin she had a barrel, which they simply allowed to roll, on the day of her funeral, from the top of the hill where she lived down to the cemetery on the plain below.

"You, you're changing into a hunting horn.

"Autumn has long been famous for its

1 A Paris hospital, formerly an asylum, on a site which originally housed a gunpowder factory, hence its name, saltpetre being a component of gunpowder.

violins[1]. You're giving it a brass instrument, several brass instruments, a whole fanfare of sobs.

"You dream, you weep.

"And what does it matter to you if the words are monotonous, as long as there are variations in the music. Well, you've left no stone unturned for the accompaniment. A little more and you would have pulled out your tibias to make flutes of them. But be careful. A skeleton very quickly breaks into pieces. So go and look at yourself in the river which serves as your mirrored wardrobe and you'll see that your body is already short on bones. It is already falling apart, its thickness that of a biscuit. Your anatomy? More inextricable than a tapeworm. Small pebbles of tears scrape your gaze. You're no more than a monstrous and ophthalmic serpent. Everyone walks over you, and I'm christening you 'Rue des Paupières-Rouges'."[2]

Biting into mid-air the man's eyes have opened wide, and his eyelashes have stretched up towards the heavens. But, in the squares,

---

1 A reference to Verlaine's poem *Chanson d'Automne,* 'Song of Autumn', in particular the lines 'The long sobs / of the violins of Autumn / pierce my heart / with monotonous languor'.
2 'Red-eyelids Street'.

the grass is dying blade by blade from diamonds of ice and, despite shoes, underwear and clothes, the seemingly most protected parts of the flesh are already cracking, as in other seasons it yields to the temptation of unripe apples, the taste of seaweed and moss, gently stretching from palate to tongue.

Previous to the tide of fog, the man, when he passed in front of the shop where the most fragile peaches lay on a bed of leaves, envied both their present and their previous life, for everything is always simple for fruits and their trees. A pity that October is not an orchard, any more than vines are the rue des Paupières-Rouges.

But since the month, with its thirty-one arms, persists in dropping its hands, the leaves, since today's waste ground is forgotten in favour of yesterday's fertility, weeks and weeks ago febrility-bearing February, brother of cherry-bearing cherry tree and plum-bearing plum tree, sprang from February's sleeping earth.

The City had neither dreamed, nor wept.

So, the street was without a name. The man had fire running down his body and strange burning tongues licking at his skin from the inside. His feet were hurting, enough to give the impression that the chilblains would soon erupt, scarlet tulips, whilst his forehead, his fingers were yielding to the snow's caress. At the front of a clockmaker's shop, on other side of the window amongst the watches and the Fix[1] jewels, on a crimson velvet slab, a tin alarm clock showed the time in a voluptuously contradictory way, whilst equally heartily the cold with its triangular blades well entrenched in the muscles, and that lava giving to the blood its consuming force, could at the same time be both cherished and feared. As, at the end of the wine harvest, the intoxication of the last rays of sun and the first cuvée are celebrated, at the same time in the icy dusk there floated the shred of a refrain:

> *February bearer of febrility.*
> *A new time. A new time.*

The right thumb and the index finger encircled the left wrist where a fairly large vein beat violently enough to impose its rhythm on the words. But one couplet was not enough. You would need couplets and couplets. Not just to reflect the glory of the new time, but also to express how its joyful opposite, eter-

---

1 A long-standing brand of French jewellery.

nity, delivers us from the present. So, after the opposite of the present, it would be the opposite of the opposite of the present. Thus, the present itself, resuscitated. One sure fact: instead of its usual cover, the dull halo, the city was beneath a zebra skin of black, white, black, at the whim of the fatality required by the body of the man, immobile on the pavement, hot, cold, hot.

Black, white, black. Hot, cold, hot. Blows to the heart, blows to the gaze. He who receives them could not tell whether they're from a large heavy club or from a sharp dagger, digging away. February, bearer of febrility, like the plum-bearing plum tree, the cherry-bearing cherry tree. Muscles, a brain, torn apart. Tortured translucency. Tormented spider's web. It's a miracle that the jostling of the young lads and lasses doesn't tear into this fragility, that on the contrary it is itself sweetness and light. A miracle too that from a trombone, already a paradox in a shop which only sells accordions and mandolins, should gush a huge bird of flame.

Suddenly, the mosaic of shade and light is abolished in the flame.

> *February bearer of febrility.*
> *A new time. A new time.*

The City, in a coquettish mood that day and perfumed like old damp newspaper, as soon as she had seen this unhoped-for phoenix thought that it would not have an unattractive effect on her chignon. She dashes into the nearest patisserie, buys vitriol meringues and dynamite biscuits and offers them to the flame-bird. But he's not so stupid, he refuses the temptation of these treacherous sweetmeats. And now the poisoner is green with rage and bent on vengeance. She shouts, gesticulates, until there's a crowd around her, and then starts a harangue:

"What you first thought was a flame, then an eagle, good people, dear idiots, is just a large turkey with rat's eyes, a skate's jaw and wings of calf's lungs with more holes in it than a woollen rug that your great-grandmother forgot to treat with naphthalene. And make sure you don't cry that it's a marvel, you the poultry seller, the fattest and most naïve of them all. Great fool! If the conjuror could really magic so many chickens and pigeons out of his handkerchief from the depths of his top hat, or the skirts of his tailcoat, you would scarcely risk becoming a millionaire. This feathered aviator coming out of a trombone, you're not going to make out that he grew out of the brass, like the mushrooms growing out of the damp earth. The bird is nothing but a filthy hooligan. Because he heard the Pope saying 'We' when he was speaking of himself, he, who likes to play the fool, wants people to call him 'Lungs', in the plural, with an s. A good-for-nothing, who doesn't even know how to breathe. A mackerel. His wife, an out-and-out example of a tart, one named 'Pleurisy'. The master of the house passes afternoons stuck at the pavement edge. The animal and the malady which serves as its female get bored. They leave his breast, their home. On with the spree! They'll kiss the little apple-pink clouds up there, colder than lemon ices. Greedy as a blackbird. But Mr Lungs won't last long. His heart is playing up. Pleurisy—a real assize court name, my good people—is poisoning him drop by drop. She'll do for him. It was she who hassled him so that he fell into the instrument, from which you saw him emerge just now, at the accordion seller's shop. He hurt himself, poor creature. He's going back into his cage, humbly. Knocks against the man's side. He's perhaps going to die between the bars of this thorax. Hark how he coughs. I myself prefer a swan's song…"

"Bon voyage," hisses the City.

The next day, it was Switzerland.

Four weeks later the calendar announced the birth of spring. Who could have believed it? Snow was persisting in covering everything with the same white lead.

The country, neither town nor village. An apiary of sick people. On their honeycomb of balconies creatures live in silence, immobility, enough to make you believe they've lost even their destinies. But after the time spent under the discipline of the late-morning chaises longues, they are allowed an hour with the gramophone.

And then the discs turn and turn.

Each person launches their own music. Laments and pizzazz intertwined, laughter in triplets and great sentimental dreams. In this tangle of tunes, no one loses the thread of his own. Neapolitan flourishes, Scottish romances, negro lispings, operatic cries, monologues and patter from the café-concerts come rushing, bumping into each other at the ever-open windows. Any song, for the person who chose it, whether it be the reediest, the weakest, spontaneously obliterates all the others.

Now, the man, when he arrived on the gramophone mountain, had not the slightest musical equipment in his luggage.

Thus, lost amid the savannah of sounds where the weakest liana is a lasso with which he who throws it, with his shortness of breath and heavy heart, strangles everything which is not the rhythm of the chosen minute, he around whom so much solitude tangled its aggressive branches over the walls did not even wish to be a blade of grass, the palest blade of grass, beneath these icy tropics of egoism.

His perpetual silence, unruffled by any pride, also despised the deceit of so-called resignation which is always certain, like an ulterior motive, that the spirit will avenge the body.

For him, at the time of the enforced rest on the honeycomb balcony, between waking and sleeping, the cascade of pine trees with its sudden hollows was never the symbol of some wonderful retribution. From the holes, amidst the waves of shadows breaking as far as the care home[1], nothing could escape which was in its lyricism or grandeur a complement to

1 'Soignoir' in the text—an invented word, but with overtones of 'caring' (soigner).

bodily decline, as green is to red. The man had no longer any rancour or spite about that, but the fact that others took pleasure in playing at being humble whilst secretly hoping that the illness would cause a miraculous spring to gush forth, that comic-opera opportunism persisting in remembering cities of legend and their golden submerged roofs, only visible to the ship-wrecked, this fact had once and for all put him on guard against the crass lies, so romantic and comforting.

The sombre ocean of leafless trees could open up, and he could roll down to the bottom of this funnel, buried in a wall of fog. His immobility which dents the cushions has already stopped warming them. His body abandoned, a ghost ship. You're sliding along like a river downhill. The horizon tips. Sleep, perhaps death... Without that inexorable pain which braked just at the right moment, at the moment of his last wisp of consciousness.

The man wakes, ready to recognise the shape of the pine trees, the exact colours of his blanket. He even, despite himself, hums the couplet to the glory of February, bearer of febrility. The idiot! Why did you shout, believe in new times, when, fibre by fibre, your muscles were tearing? Pain, that bitch, he let it bite into his flesh. Accustomed since childhood to torments, their garlands, crowns, chains around suffering breasts, foreheads, wrists, if he has sung *February bearer of febrility,* it's because he hoped, just like the young friends nowadays disparaged, that the storm—a mix of ice and flames, would give this thought a rarer electricity, which he'd enjoyed imagining being heralded by the thunder of his fits of coughing.

Now, on the mountain of gramophones, at dawn on the first morning, when the nurse came in for the alcohol and cold water rub, he understood the vanity of all this imagery.

His flesh fearful, his heart impatient of the dawning day, he found himself once again subjected to the perfidy of its pale gleams, abandoned amongst the swamps of a hazy sun. Between the deceitful muslins of the dawn and the curtains he searched for an object, something precise to stare at. The ironwork of the balcony saved him from sinking into the bog. Today, every few months in the rue des Paupières-Rouges the same threatening scraps of fog trail.

But this time, not the least lifebuoy. The man yields to the blurriness.

His teeth chatter, his cheeks grow pale making his eyes roll. He's nothing but a wreck. He forgets the given name, the surname, which have designated him for twenty-seven years. From now on and until the end of his days he will be Mr Vagualame[1]. Mr Vagualame for good, for real, with a big heart in crumbs into which the old witch of the fairgrounds, Madame de Rosalba, will be able to plant as many and as absurd arrows as she pleases. Already he's looking for the redhead with whom to make a blue child. Wasted effort. Women have no more colour than the mauve of waning violets, on their lips, on their cheeks. Mr Vagualame, this evening, will have to make do with a creature who has suddenly appeared, as good as naked and rustling with tulle, with such a low neckline that he feels cold for her and offers her his coat, his scarf. The woman, refusing them, spontaneously introduces herself.

"I'm Yolande, Yolande the beauty, a femme fatale. Let us be friends."

Mr Vagualame kisses Yolande's hand.

He then understands why her shoulders, her bosom are not suffering from this icy fog.

1 Avoir du vague à l'âme—to feel melancholic; hence Mr Melancholia earlier, but from now on he is Mr Vagualame.

The quivering of her dress, the pallor her skin with its lack of colour, are not the only things making her seem like the cousin of fishes, for her blood itself has no greater heat than a trout's. Just as well, for Mr Vagualame has his usual high temperature. On one side an excess, on the other lack of temperature. There will be an average.

Yolande has a fan. She opens it, and to Vagualame, who makes her a very polite comment about it, explains: "I love trinkets made from rare and subtle materials. This one is from glass paper, simply set in cloves. I'm the opposite of Mimi Patata who always wants showiness. She's old-fashioned, poor thing. But just now, there's the chink of fake jewellery coming through the fog straight towards us; I bet it's her. It is. Hello Mimi…"

In love with the figure two, between two ages, two wines, two bars when she dances, two notes when she sings, the star of the Folies-Bergère had yesterday evening a great success at the dress rehearsal dancing the zig zag which she interpreted in the most natural way. The height of happiness. A Maharajah was introduced to her whose thirty wives had given birth all on the same day some twenty-five years ago, each to a pair of twins. So the Swedish[1] twins no longer have the same value. Let them obey to the letter or else a little trip to the domains of the papa Maharajah, and Mimi will have the thirty pairs of young and handsome Hindus. Do you hear that, you twins?

Appearing out of some patch of shadow the twins smile in unison at their communal mistress who feigns indifference.

Yolande orders:

"Let's go to my place."

---

1 'Dalécarliens' in the text — Dalecarlian is a group of dialects spoken in Dalarna County, Sweden.

II

At Yolande's.—The Rosalba woman understood nothing of it.—The incredible truth.—The living dead woman.—The fakir.—The apartment bull.—The rat weighing fifty kilos.—Yolande's past, her life when she was known as Myrto-Myrta.—The Austrian Court during the war.—The shady side of spying.—Myrto-Myrta is denounced by a mysterious man, whom she met and loved one evening in Seville.—Court martial.—The Vincennes execution post.—How the touch of the fakir resurrects her.—She becomes Yolande.—The fakir does his work.—Sad memories.—Before Myrto-Myrta there was little Camille, the daughter of a coachman.—A childhood in Picpus.—Pauline, Camille's twin.—The song of the pigtail-pullers.—Evil influence of the word "prépuce"[1].—A coachman father cracks open his skull on the edge of a pavement.—A widow who leads the high life.—In which Camille and Pauline, her twin, raped by the Italian, their mother's lover, demand more,

---

1 "Foreskin".

more.—They are exiled to the Trône fair[1], to their godmother's, the flea trainer.—Crying "pique-puce" the future Myrto-Myrta-Yolande decimates the menagerie. —Dreams and remorse.—Rachel, ruined, leaves with her goddaughters in search of the widow.—The widow, also ruined, beaten and deceived by the Italian,   uses the profile which she owes to well-administered punches, in order to change into Madame Dante.—Rachel becomes extra lucid.—Her metamorphosis into Madame Rosalba.—In which we learn that Mimi Patata has since puberty been in love with male and female twins and that Pauline, the sister of Camille-Myrto-Myrta-Yolande, is the mother of a redhead-ed daughter.—It is this redhead, a symbol for her of perfection, that the naïve Rosalba predicts to her clients when she wishes to please them.

At Yolande's.

Dinner hurried through in two speeds, two movements because of Mimi who does the zig zag straight after the interval.

So, at the time of the dessert she gets up and leaves, followed by her 'twins'.

Yolande and Mr Vagualame, left alone, go to sit in the salon, Yolande in her cathe-

1 La Foire du Trône in Paris: the oldest traditional fun-fair in France.

dra, where she towers over Mr Vagualame crouched down on one of Abd el-Kater's grandson's stools. With an imperious gesture the mistress of herein indicates the Gothic-Arabic wonders and concludes:

"Madame de Rosalba has not deceived you, monsieur, at least not about the furnishings and trinkets of my precious collection. Thanks to her, even before you came in, you had a very precise idea of the works of art that it pleased me gather between these walls. But your crystal-gazer lied and will be punished for lying about everything concerning my love-life, my friends and the so-called debauchery which they and I gave ourselves up to together. I know Madame de Rosalba and always know what she's going to say. How? Why? That's my business. She, on the other hand, knows nothing about me. That is to say, nothing important. The truth, monsieur, my truth would kill her, so set is she on her claim to have the most mysterious knowledge. Nor would she be the only one, for understanding my secret requires solid intelligence and nerves, rather more solid than, for example, those of our good Patata and her twins. One single time I almost let it out. It was to the Prince of Wales. At the last moment I drew back. His Highness would have been torn between the affection which I like to think he has for me and the duties of his birth. In short, I spared the prince the ordeal of this Cornelian dilemma. Without suspecting the mystery of my life, one of those mysteries that make spirits sink, topple cities, ruin civilisations, he continues to haunt this house, to give himself up as in the past to the innocent pleasures of the broderie anglaise. He has even just completed a large bedspread which he gave me as a present and which I shall show you later. That said, since you think of yourself as a strong man, monsieur, hold on to your stool with both hands for, finally, to you I shall confess everything. Forgot about the wreck that I snatched from the rue des Paupières-Rouges. Become again who you were before, the navigator of the crystal submarine with flags of pride. Find again this boat which wounded the rocks. It was of your stature and its made-to-measure transparency feared neither torpedo rays nor sharks with razor-sharp teeth. Stretched out once again along the hold, explore the depths. The rays knocking their mauve jaws against the ship, invisible to them, will give your dreams a crown of orchids, cold as the hands that the proud Yolande deigns to tie around your forehead. Close your eyes, Vagualame. From the depths emerges a voice. The voice of Yolande. And Yolande is the mystery woman. Of her, you know only a first name. Just now, in the rue des Paupières-Rouges, you saw from a distance Mimi and her twins coming. But as for Yolande, how did she spring from the pavement?"

"Sprang from the pavement?" repeated Vagualame.

"…Sprang like the iris springs which its adorers a hundred times—what am I saying? A thousand times, thousands and thousands of times, told her she was. Iris. She dresses only in black tulle."

And she explains:

"My cheeks, my lips, my whole face, my neck, my arms are white, white, white; and my whole person is white, more than white, colourless, bloodless, beneath the make-up and dress with which I have covered them. The only authentic colour is the stone grey of the eyes. My skin is smooth like that of plants. And without heat, too. Do you want check it? Touch the fingers, the lips. All contacts are allowed. Come. Come, my darling. Take advantage of the opportunity. You won't find everywhere a dead woman who talks and moves. I promised you the truth. I have just told it to you. I am a dead woman. And not the only unbelievable being of this house. Follow me, I shall introduce you to the fakir, to the apartment bull, to the rat which weighs fifty kilos.

"First, the fakir. He's here. Let's open the door. Good evening fakir. You'll find him a bit shrivelled for your liking. Well, fifty years with no food, no drink, without moving. He closed his fists when he was twenty. He's seventy now and has never opened them. His nails have pierced his palms. Well, my dear man, it's to this calm old man that I owe the fact that I'm not rotting away in a coffin. My body feeds on contact with him. Of course, I remain deprived of the warmth and the colours of the living. But everything works out. My arms are well known, I only need to paint myself from head to toe after my ablutions. You're wondering how a fakir was able to restore speech, movement, intelligence to the dead woman I confess to having been. I myself have no idea. A secret from India that Europe cannot explain. The fakir was with a rich family of Pondicherry. You think that he didn't cost millions for his upkeep. Nevertheless his owners, suddenly impoverished, got rid of him. A man who loved me brought him to me. He knew the way to make use of him, which anyway is very simple. One application of this great visionary on the skin, just a small amount, and this gathering of psychic forces restores the most vital attributes of life. So, I pass him all over my body, all over my face. You have to undertake this little procedure at least twice every day. Whilst travelling, for example, that's not very practical. Even though he's so shrivelled the poor dear doesn't fit into an ordinary suitcase. You have to put him in the goods wagon. I had a small trunk made for him where he's as happy as can be. Doesn't stop me always being afraid that he'll get broken or lost. One day, at the station in Florence, he couldn't be found, imagine that. Finally, someone brought him back. Just in time. It's true, I've never had any other problems. Good little fakir. Not rushing around, not making a noise. And that oriental silence. What an affront to European slovenliness. You can imagine how I thank from the bottom of my heart the man who brought him back. He was an Englishman from an excellent family with a castle in Scotland, a villa in Beaulieu, and a yacht and all the trappings. And what manners, my little friend. In the evenings, for dinner, always in a dinner jacket or suit even if it was just us two. No hairy paws. Skin like velvet, with muscles rippling beneath. All the women were mad about him. Still today I swoon just remembering him. Imagine how I fell head over heels when I met him. At that time I didn't need a fakir to be able to move arms and legs. My name was Myrto-Myrta. I had warm blood. I danced. Not the zig zag, of course, but real dances with chassés, half-turns, points, splits, Spanish dances, Greek, Neapolitan, Arabic, Gipsy, Chinese, Tibetan, and Negro dances, from the quirky to ballet. There was something for every taste. The war interrupted my performances. The Englishman, who in order to maintain his way of life, had had to accept the propositions of the Intelligence Service, drew me into espionage. We both had as much activity as appetite. Serving both sides was kid's stuff. There wasn't a payroll we weren't on.

"In Vienna, going under the names of Baron and Baroness von Veidt, we could enter the Court at any time. Old Franz-Joseph who, despite his age, was still often eyeing up the women, showed me so much respect that soon the whole city reckoned I was his mistress. I let them think it. The Emperor was not at all demanding. He was in heaven if you just pinched his chin whilst softly singing: I'm holding on to your little beard.

"As gently as I could I stroked his wrinkled forehead, the famous whiskers. Often too we would imagine great wild goat hunts in the Tyrol, once the war was over. I had even ordered some leather shorts for myself. As thanks for all my kindness, he would tell me the secrets of the Hapsburgs and the Empire. I've heard lots of them, you know. Enough to write books and books. When he had opened wide his old heart to me, he would drop off to sleep with a blissful smile on his lips. Deep down I loved him, dear old Franzy. But you think I wasn't going to waste my time going soft. Everything he rattled on about was worth its weight in gold, and scarcely had he closed his eyes than I went back home where my darling and I would be busy making our reports. Alas, the darling received an order from London to leave for India. For me, I had to stay in Austria. A bad moment to live through. Franzy would repeat himself. He had fixed ideas. He was declining. He died. I went into mourning. There was nothing to be had from his successor who loved his lawful wife and didn't stop having children with her. My Myrto-Myrta sold to the Viennese the strategic plans of Clermont-Ferrand and Brive-la-Gaillarde and as she had the means to pay for some little holidays for herself she packed her bags and went. And it was Spain and its castanets, as the Mimi's review said. A bad idea. The Englishman wouldn't be back for months and months. Myrto-Myrta was getting bored. In Grenada one evening, in the gardens of the Alhambra, a handsome young man offered her some pinks. They kissed. They went back to the hotel. They made love. Oof. They made love again. Myrto-Myrta didn't forget her darling. But his replacement didn't displease her at all. He asked her some questions. She went for a few small false confidences, so insignificant, so well wrapped up, that he certainly didn't pick up on anything. He played at being secretive. She baptised him Mr Mystery. One day Mr Mystery had to go back to France. He begged her to follow him. She agreed. Now they were in a large bed in Paris. Mr Mystery told how he was born on a Sunday at midday."

"And then?" asked Myrto-Myrta, who had never liked glib tall stories.

"'Then,' replied Mr Mystery, 'this is the then, Madame. Like all those who are born on a Sunday at midday I surmise, I feel, I know what someone wants to hide from me.'

"Mr Mystery clenched his teeth. Myrto-Myrta was frightened by the small yellow marks suddenly lighting up his eyes. She tried to get up, to run away. But he was already twisting her wrists. She cried out. He tightened his grip and she howled. He sneered:

"'No need to be frightened, Madame Franz-Joseph's mistress, the police will come to save you from me...'

"And there in fact were the cops. They dragged the woman from the sheets. She panicked. The man got up. He smirked:

"'You knew how to pretend, Madame, but you were not the cleverest. Allow me to introduce myself. Captain X... of military intelligence, whose mission was to put into the hands of the French authorities the traitorous woman who has been selling the strategic plans of Clermont-Ferrand and Brive-la-Gaillarde. I thank you, Madame, for having made the grim mission of a soldier so agreeable.'"

Just remembering the captain's taunt and the words with which he derided her the former Myrto-Myrta, Yolande, still today becomes exasperated. She takes Vagualame as a witness.

"Have you ever seen such a shady character? And who could have guessed the real face of Mr Mystery beneath the mask of a well-built handsome young chap? It was no good my knowing about espionage, I was done for. Mr Mystery accompanied me to Saint-Lazare, where my only vengeance was to spit in his face as a farewell. So with my anger thus assuaged I decided to accept unflinchingly all the ordeals to come, telling myself: 'I played, I lost.' So, it was the same callous face I saw, in my dungeon, in the office of the investigating magistrate, at the court martial, when they read out the sentence condemning me to capital punishment. My lawyer had written to India, and on the eve of the very day when I was to be executed I learned that my darling would return the next day with a top-of-the-range fakir and knowledge of how to use him. It seemed I was saved. I danced, I sang. The sisters thought I was mad. Let them go to hell! I didn't close my eyes all night. Finally the day of atonement dawned, as the priest said who arrived at daybreak. But out with the fellow in black! I prefer the traditional glass of rum to his *De profundis*. I get dressed up. To see me, you'd think that I'm off to a wedding. Black silk dress with a large pleated ruffle, polished shoes. Open-work stockings, as was the fashion at the time. Over my shoulders a silver fox fur. A huge hat of aubergine velvet, with a large feather in the same shade. A few jewels. No diamonds, no rubies. Nothing but pearls, a sapphire on my left ring finger, my gold and crystal Lalique locket, and finally a lorgnette. They came to get me. A moment please. A little dusting of powder and I was ready. The mirrors of the Third Republic don't have mirrors... There. Don't get impatient. I'm coming, I'm coming.

"The execution ground. I got down from the van which had taken me there. My defence lawyer offered me his arm. We walked between two rows of helmeted, armed soldiers. Thanks to the lorgnette which gave me a presence, and the aubergine ostrich feather, I was like a queen inspecting her troops. We arrived at the execution post: they attached me. The clumsy idiots crumpled my dress. Too bad. There would be others. I did not want to remove my hat. I refused to let them blindfold me. My lawyer kissed my hand. The platoon commander was so flustered that I myself called out: 'Fire!' They fired. I fell. I was dead.

"My resurrection.

"My body was reclaimed, apparently by my family. Actually, I was taken to the home of my darling. My eyes had just opened again and I saw my incomparable lover running the fakir over my naked body. This contact healed the wounds and reawakened my senses. The lawyer was at my bedside. He introduces to me a very smart little old man, a spiritual doctor, one of his friends, who had come to supervise the operation which that lovely Englishman intended to carry out with his own hands. The spiritualist was full of joy, for it seems my aura had just that minute returned. Soon I would be able to prance about, laugh, love. However, I would never again have warmth or colour. I would have to get used to that. It was expected. My defence lawyer, who never forgets anything, offered me a box of make-up. My darling started singing *God save the King* and pushing the fakir at me with all his strength. The work completed, the lawyer and the doctor left. My darling put the little chap on the edge of the table and quickly, in a flash, undressed. Bang, jacket in one corner, braces in another. All of it off: waistcoat, trousers, shirt, shoes, tie. That beautiful pink male flesh was all the more wildly attractive compared with the parchment stretched over the bones of the shrivelled little man.

"To your good health, fakir. We'll go with a jolly little zig zag." And you'll have nothing to complain about, with such a lovely couple at your feet, he the lecherous Englishman, she being caressed by him and being called "his dear little talking and moving dead woman," and swooning with passion. They embrace tightly enough to break their bones.

Their bad luck!

Myrto-Myrta forgot that she was no warmer than ice. A whisky drinker, rubbing up against an ice floe, lying flat upon an iceberg, rolling around on it, runs a big risk of a stroke. Why did she not think of that as she dreamed of melting like snow in his arms, between the legs of a volcano. He suddenly flared up, red, blue, violet, black and after this rainbow spasm became white and cold, as white, as cold, as she. He'd stopped moving. So he was dead. Myrto-Myrta took the fakir, ran him over all his body as she had seen him do for her. Ouch! Her resurrection had emptied out the poor little chap. And she, who would have wanted so much, in her turn, to save her saviour! In the time it would take for the fakir to recharge his powers, her darling would be too long dead to ever be returned to her. And then she would herself, in less than twelve hours from now, have to be refakirised. Of course she would willingly miss her turn, but if the sacrifice miraculously proved not to be futile, the tender Anglo-Saxon, who had never ceased swearing that without Myrto-Myrta his existence would seem to him to be the worst of evils, would not know what to do without the life which she would deprive herself off by renouncing her own and indispensable pittance of psychic strength.

She just did not know what to do. She cried, she howled. And the fakir wasn't moving. Prayers, insults, slaps in the face, sobs, threats. Nothing worked. Not a foot or paw budged. Yolande would have happily thrown him out of the window. But she had no time to lose. She put the shrivelled thing back on the table, telephoned the lawyer. He arrived with the spiritualist doctor who could only confirm the Englishman's death.

They quickly dressed and painted Myrto-Myrta who left with the fakir under her arm, wrapped in newspapers.

Another life was beginning.

Whilst Myrto-Myrta was facing the firing squad, the Englishman had had the excellent idea of passing the time by cashing the large cheque, payment for his services in Austria and India. So, as once resuscitated she had taken his wallet and a few locks of his hair as a souvenir, she had some money. One more thing. She needed a new civil status and henceforth would be known as Yolande of Scabbiness. And another thing. Soon, because Scabbiness lent itself to nicknames and because the gossips dubbed her The Scabby One, she would be just Yolande. Because of her attachment to family and friends she renewed her links to those who were dear to Myrto-Myrta, whom they thought to be dead and would not recognise. First, the Prince of Wales. The English never ask indiscreet questions. And then the crown prince would not go nit-picking and would not even listen to the incredible story. As for the Patata woman who had been close since childhood to Myrto-Myrta, and as there had very often been rivalry between the two ladies, since she had believed the other one buried she took her vengeance. And often Yolande had to suffer a flood of calumnies, unable to interrupt their flow. She listened, with clenched teeth, not breathing a word but nonetheless thinking:

"What a great coward that Patata is. One day or another she'll learn the cost of attacking the memory of a departed person. Spread your bile, my dear. Yolande will get her own back."

The far-seeing Rosalba suspected nothing, no more than did the sister of the former Myrto-Myrta, her stepbrother, her niece. The niece, the stepbrother and above all the sister, her twin—Mr Vagualame would already know all of this little family if the resuscitated woman had kept to a strict chronological order in telling her tale. But even if you have your head screwed on, so many dramas always finish by turning it upside down and our Yolande has simply harnessed the cab before the old nag, as her father the coachman used to say, but with fairly rigorous intelligence, a spirit of realism, adapting for city folk the old agricultural cliché of putting the cart before the horse.

Before Myrto-Myrta—already a pseudonym—there was a charming child who had been baptised Camille. Pauline was Camille's twin. Rather a Cornelian name, no doubt, but one which the fatal outcome of things would justify, although the father, who did not intend his daughters to become either swashbucklers along the lines of Horace's Curiace, or drinkers of holy water à la Polyeuctus[1], would never have intended to indicate that they would know the tragic and grandiose fate of two lovers torn apart as was the case, for example, with the narrator on the day when, naked, dishevelled, in tears she ran from the depleted fakir to the already cold Englishman, from the Englishman to the fakir, without finding a satisfactory solution for the simple reason that there was not, and could never be, a satisfactory solution.

The coachman, out of legitimate professional pride, had called his first-born who had died young 'Urbaine'. For those who followed he had therefore decided they would be Camille and Pauline, since, after the Urbaine, the two most renowned cab companies were one, the Camille, the other, the Pauline.

The coachman and his family lived in Picpus, which fate made a pretext for the tragedy which, through the death of one of them, changed the lives of the others.

At school the girls were teased:

1 Horace and Polyeuctus (Polyeucte) are the title characters in two of Corneille's plays.

"Look, here come the girls who pick the pops."

In the streets, the boys pulled their pigtails singing:

> *Picky pop*
> *Pretty pussies*
> *Pretty prick*
> *Is getting picky*
> *Pick a poppet*
> *Not a patsy.*[1]

Because of the association with pickiness, the innocent girls thought that pretty prick was a fancy way of saying: grocer. One afternoon when her mother had sent her to buy two sous-worth of mustard, the future friend of the Prince of Wales, already keen on pomp and esoteric expressions, having curtseyed to the shop worker who had served her, said pompously: "Goodbye and thank you, pretty prick." The server liked a bit of hanky-panky. He offered her three acid drops, one red, one yellow, one green, so that she repeated three times: "Thank you, pretty prick." The cashier who had watched this ploy pricked up her ears. Her son, a lad of ten, had as it happened

1 The original: *Pique puce / Mes pucelles / Mon prépuce / A du sel / Pour la celle / Sans puce.*

just been circumcised in connection with some nasty habits, and in her dictionary of sensuality foreskin indicated a puerile vice. She got a pen holder out of its box, pinched along with a majestic false chignon.

"Do you take the grocery for a cat-house, Augusse?"

"Quiet you old dear."

"Rude man! And you, you little piece of filth, hurry up and clear off. What a dreadful thing. Not even finished growing and already a trollop."

The father arrived, very proud upon his cab.

Camille cried: "Papa, papa, she called me a trollop."

A whip cracked.

"So you want to dance, grumpy old woman?"

The cashier was hurt. A crowd gathered. The local pharmacist brought some eau de mélisse. A policeman took aside the coach-man who had got down from his seat and swore that despite his resistance he would take him to the police station. Fisticuffs. A top hat of boiled leather rolled into the gutter and the father fell so unluckily that he cracked his skull open on the edge of the pavement.

Taken to the hospital, he died the next day.

The widow sold the cab, bought herself a pink corset, some fancy knickers, twelve beribboned nightdresses and set up home with a Neapolitan, a real tomcat, who in bed was worth at least a hundred times the coachman. But scarcely had she turned her back than the Italian speedily seduced the twins who demanded "More, more". The Italian responded suitably to the chorus of the two insatiable girls. But at that moment the widow returned, who thought very astutely that a man was not like a melon, a fruit made, as Bernardin de Saint-Pierre said, to be shared by all the family.

So, Mr Macaroni, who has the keys to the mirrored wardrobe where the cash is hidden? There are still three quarters of the old cart and the broken-down nag to be guzzled. So you have to choose. The widow likes nooky, of course, but she's not up for being pimped and having fun made of her into the bargain. Wait a bit, geezer. The widow is on the ball. And then, she has some advantages that make her really up to it. Yesterday, on the Madeleine-Bastille bus, a fancy-looking man with a blond moustache, polished shoes, a starched collar, was happy enough to pinch her bottom. She still has a bruise on her right buttock to show for it. So you can imagine that she wouldn't have any trouble finding another man, with her bum and these beefy arms which squeeze tight the handsome lads, but take note you big fool, she's quite capable of giving a good beating to the filthy louts who disrespect her. That's not all. We know you're keen on rumpy-pumpy. You're so nuts about holes you'd think your grandmother was a mole. So it's sure you haven't forgotten your nice surprise the first time you explored the widow. See now. You're licking your lips just remembering her gripping it like a nutcracker. Nothing more need be said. We understand each other. When you are well on the way, Mr Macaroni, with your mouth on her mouth and that thing of yours swelling up down below in the hollow between her legs, both naked, the little muscle deep inside which she can play with as she wishes, that's all you need to feel you're in paradise. Such good work, enough for you to put your feet up. So then try to get these tricks out of anaemic youngsters. The insipid twins for example. If you really want to, you can always take them. But you'll have been warned. They have their own shirts and clobber. Not a bean. And too young to be on the streets. As you yourself haven't ever had any other job than walking around offering plaster statuettes to passers-by you three won't be much of a success. Don't tell the widow.

She has a nice little number, she knows very well that she's onto a sure thing. So all you have to do is ask her forgiveness, kiss her, pamper her. You're scarcely to be pitied, you with your dark brooding good looks. You cling to each other, you keel over, and the bed is already sinking beneath your embrace. What a tangling of thighs! The twins weep tears of rage. Avenged, their mother delights in her victory as sweet to her heart as the curly hair, the lips, the long fluttering eyelashes and especially, very quietly, protected by the soft skin of his neck, a chignon of muscles are to the caress of her fingers.

Forgiven, the Neapolitan gets up, tidies up his clothes which have been slightly dis-arranged by the exploits which have brought about his rehabilitation. He returns with his mandolin and sings "O sole mio". Then, from the body of the most satisfied of the widows who live the high life, as if from her belly button as she buttons up her bodice, emerges a sparkling semi-circle of frost and ice like the feathers of a peacock strutting its stuff. As for the twins, it's impossible even for them not to wonder at these tenorinades[1] coming from a mouth the shape of a hen's bottom, like eggs whose shells break to give birth to the flimsy chicks of a water colour, which of course are not the simple swallows of fine days humming:

> *On your breast, my beauty.*
> *I shall rest,*

but the aerial brothers of Japanese fish, a small flock fluttering sentimentally in the sky of two pairs of eyes. Now, leaning over the edge of the eyelids, vertiginously, these transparent humming birds fall, and, in their fall, melt with fear.

In other words, the twins are in tears.

Their mother, who could not bear to have such a pure pleasure spoiled for her, grumbles:

"Silly geese, instead of bugging us with your moaning you'd have done better to look after your pussies…"

Pretty prick, pussies, a single family in which everyone is tickling underarms and the soles of their feet. Camille giggles. A nervous giggle. She jumps up onto her chair. A St Vitus

---

1 This appears to be an invented word to describe the crooning sounds of the tenor's song.

dance of flesh and bones. The Italian thinks she's mocking him and throws his mandolin out of the window. This life can't go on. Camille and Pauline will go to live with their godmother, cousin Rachel, whose caravan has pride of place in all the Parisian fairgrounds.

It's now that the future Yolande begins to get a taste for grandeur, and to dream of the beautiful life. She is drawn to it by the very surroundings of the camp, and especially by the flamboyant personality of her godmother.

With her huge beige felt hat with its right side pinned up by an amethyst and wrought iron gemstone, shaded by an azure feather around its rim which descends like a waterfall over her back and thighs, with her green velvet short jacket and her long skirt with its train tailored from the astrologer's robe of her late husband (patterned with gold stars on a red background), with her riding crop, her large necklaces and zinc bracelets, her brash make-up and violet leather silver-braided Russian boots which she shows as she lifts her petticoat with a gloved hand, Rachel has a deceptive look of Mlle de Montpensier. The sateen of an old eiderdown and the bright red cotton of some disused curtains have provided her with the means to make page costumes for her goddaughters and at eight o'clock every weekday evening, and in the early afternoon on Sundays and Thursdays, they come with great pomp down the four steps leading from the caravan to the pavement. The pages lay a dark red plush cloth over a high table, whilst the look-alike Montpensier comes and goes, like a diabolical dethroned amazon but one who hopes that a stallion with its nightmarish nostrils and its hooves of fire will suddenly emerge from between the paving slabs.

And why not?

The late astrologer, from his reading of the Great Bear, had finally learned there that one can come back to earth several times. He, the time before last, had been Napoleon, not he of [18]70[1], no, but the great one, the only one, who went to Russia *pedibus cum jambis*[2] with a great army, just to stretch his legs, and made only one mistake in his life when after years and years he left his dear old Josephine and impregnated the Austrian Emperor's daughter. Rachel, without ever having known such

1 Napoleon III was the first president of France from 1848 to 1852 and the emperor of the French from 1852 to 1870.
2 On foot, walking.

glory, nevertheless at her previous appearance had been a woman whose name she has now forgotten but a famous person somewhere between Cléo de Mérode[1] and Queen Amélie of Portugal. That is why she now wears so many stars on her dress. But the most star-spangled silks are faded by the rain, frayed by the dust, dulled by time and the steed worthy of her fancy finery does not often make an appearance. She must again, as always, put off the wonderful and infernal horseback ride and resign herself to the garnet-red plush-covered table, since the necessities of existence have made of her a flea tamer.

And now as it happens the twins/pages arrive bringing the tiny wild creatures in their appropriately sized cages: "Roll up gentlemen, ladies, and you too, soldiers and children's maids. Fleas, yes, ordinary fleas, are going to dance, play the violin, pull wheelbarrows, do the housework, drive around in cars. As intelligent as the architect who built the Eiffel Tower, as gay as larks, pretty as pictures. So roll up, gentlemen, ladies, and you too, soldiers and children's maids...."

Whilst Rachel intones her sales patter, banging her riding whip against the ground,

---

1 A French dancer of the Belle Epoque.

Camille hums quietly to herself the song of the pigtail-pullers:

> *Picky pop*
> *Pretty pussies*
> *Pretty prick*
> *Is getting picky*
> *Pick a poppet*
> *Not a patsy*

She has frightened herself just by pronouncing the words pretty prick, ever since by the most evil magic of its silken syllables her father the coachman cracked open his skull on the pavement kerb. But at night, whilst Rachel sleeps, she gets up to go secretly, to the sound of picky pop, to tickle her godmother's menagerie with the point of a needle or a pin.

She gives herself up to it, before, during and afterwards for, once back in bed and sleeping, she enjoys a dream which, mixing fear and remorse, is better than lemon for someone who likes to grind their teeth.

Rachel, a greater charlatan than ever, has struck a match against the back of her hand and the whole of the fairground is lit up by the fire of her vengeance. In the dream the

guilty woman sees herself suddenly transformed into a woman of wax, stretched out
on a violet velvet bed at the entrance to the
Dupuytren Museum[1], her torso very delicately naked. But with two pairs of breasts, one
beneath the other. The widow, the Italian, all
the Picpus residents file past. When everyone
has left the flocks of fairground animals are
led out to pasture by a gruesome shepherdess,
also made of wax, holding an English book
and with a large straw hat flapping in the
wind, a pair of tortoiseshell spectacles on her
pointed fox's muzzle, wearing a frilly bodice
but with nothing on between her belt and her
feet, which nevertheless is not many metres in
length since the lovable lady-monster who has
no legs has her ankles welded to her thighs.
This gruesome shepherdess, a great traveller
who has experience of people and things and
knows that wooden horses don't feed on grass,
comes up to the glass-topped casket where the
beautiful woman with four breasts is lying and
with a blow of her unbreakable head shatters
the glass protection. Then the varnished cattle
rush up, tear apart the body of soft paraffin
wax, get drunk on the blood which is more

1 A Paris museum of wax and anatomical items and
specimens illustrating diseases and malformations.

and better perfumed than mouthwash and although it is still dark night, a sudden sun bursts out, simultaneously star and cloud, and then its light abruptly changes into a hail of daggers, its most inexorable blades flaming and converging on the target of violet velvet, whose miserable and bloody fragment will soon be, in the fading and empty night, the sole and final vestige of the universe.

Every morning the flea tamer finds corpses, cripples. The survivors, overwhelmed with sorrow and foreboding, lose all their verve, all their sparkle. One evening the last survivor of the corps de ballet is trying to dance all by herself but despite Rachel humming her favourite tune from Coppelia the poor thing has no life left in her legs. She knows she will be dead by the next day's dawn, assassinated by a hand unknown to all (except Camille, of course). And Rachel, to demonstrate her distress, will remove her star-studded dress. The fancy hat, the Russian boots and the green bodice are replaced by a shabby skirt, a loose black jacket and a hood. The twins take back the rags of their previous life. The godmother and her goddaughters, three paupers, go off to seek help from the widow.

"The widow!" cries the concierge. "But you're not up to date. The widow is far away if she's still going. She's moved on, changed her habits, and even her name."

"She's married her macaroni," Rachel supposes.

"Married? Madame is joking. They don't care about mayors and priests. The widow is called Mme Dante now. Why? Go and ask her. Here's her new address, in Les Batignolles."

And indeed, in Les Batignolles, on a door at the address indicated, there is a visiting card announcing:

Mme DANTE
PREDICTS THE FUTURE

"What luck! She's going to tell our fortunes," says the dreamy Rachel.

The former widow, Mme Dante herself, opens the door and without taking the time to say hello:

"You wouldn't have recognised me, eh? Don't look at me so insistently, you twins. And you, cousin, you can't get over it either.

It's my nose. It's retroussé. It won't drip any more. It's the fault of that blessed Italian. When he'd cleaned me out, down to the last penny, he took to beating me, so hard and so often that I'm scarred for life. One day when he was in a good mood he showed me one of his statues.

"'Your portrait,' he said to me.

"'What, that old thing who could scratch her nose with her chin?'

"'A bit more courtesy please. It's not an old woman, but the greatest poet of my beloved Italy, Dante. Since I broke your nose you could be taken for his daughter, and you can thank me for arranging the portrait for you, Mme Dante. It's better to be Mme Dante than the widow anybody…

"As the macaroni was scarcely selling any of his plaster fellows out in the streets he persuaded Mme Dante to leave Picpus, an unhappy place. So she rented a place here, at Les Batignolles, bought some tarot cards, learned how to tell the cards. Predicting the future, no problem…

"You want to know your future Rachel? For you, it's free. You're the queen of clubs. I take you out of the pack. You cut the pack with your left hand. Then, choose a card. Put it on top. Another one to the right. And another one to the left. A last one underneath. What has power over you: the knave of clubs, the mystery. What you're sure of: eight of diamonds, a short journey. What you're afraid of: ace of spades, a thorn in your heart. What you trample underfoot: seven of spades, your worries. Cover the ace of spades. Two cards. Perfect. Knave of spades: you've been betrayed my Rachel, but finally ten of hearts. You can be happy. Joy, joy, joy all along the line. Your bad luck will make your happiness. Now, choose one more card, to put onto the seven of spades: ace of hearts. You win, my Rachel, you win."

Rachel is exultant: "The knave of clubs, the mystery. Eight of diamonds, a short journey. It couldn't be better. The Neuilly fair starts next week. I'm at la Nation at the moment. So I'll cross Paris with the caravan. The thorn in the heart, that's my dead fleas. The betrayal, that again is the assassination of my fleas. But I'm energetic. I'll get on top of my unhappiness. I'll trample on it, and that's how I'll win."

"You're forgetting the ten of hearts, ungrateful woman. Since your fleas are dead, I'll explain the mystery to you, the knave of clubs who has power over you. You too are going to be a teller of cards. You will always follow the fairs (eight of diamonds, a short journey). But the red skirt with the gold stars, the green jacket, the big felt hat, the sky-blue riding habit, all the trappings which suit you so well will go much better, let's agree on it, on a fortune-teller than on a flea trainer. Off you go, cousin. As for me, I'm taking back my daughters. That miserable macaroni abandoned me, last week, for an old rich woman. I'm no longer a lover, I'm no longer a woman, I'm going back to being a mother."

So Rachel predicts the future in the fairs, and Mme Dante in Les Batignolles. Every morning the latter goes to the Monceau park to gather ivy to make crowns which she arranges around a headband over her forehead, the nape of her neck, her ears. The Italian has left her the bust of his national poet. She has placed it on the mantelpiece of her consulting room, and before beginning her predictions never misses presenting it to her clients:

"The poet Dante, my grandfather."

Upon the early death of Mme Dante Rachel sells the caravan and takes over from her. It is she herself who, under the name of Mme Rosalba, is responsible for shaking Mr Vagualame and, to make up to him for the misty greyness of the day, for promising him a redheaded wife and a blue child.

※

Back with their mother, the twins started dance classes at the Opera House. Identical in height and features they were nonetheless very different in manner and bearing: Pauline sentimental and soft, Camille with enough devilry for two, and although having no more fleas to picky pop remained faithful to her torturous perversion, biting dogs, scratching cats and dreaming of giving a head cold or a sore throat to the air currents themselves. At this time Mimi Patata was also learning some dance steps. Already keen on twosomes she fell in love with the twins. They became insep- arable. So much so that they were nicknamed the Three Graces: Pauline, the tender grace; Camille the cruel grace; Patata the Parisian grace.

At that time the great King Behanzin of Abyssinia came to Paris. The three graces danced at the Elysée Palace. Behanzin only had eyes for the cruel grace. Then began the brilliant and tragic destiny of Myrto-Myrta. The Parisian grace joined the troupe of nude women at the Folies-Bergère, where she worked her way up to captain. As for the tender grace, her godmother Rachel-Rosalba, who had made friends in Les Batignolles and knew an architect, managed to marry her to this constructor who thought himself a Solness[1] and dreamt up strange buildings which refused to remain standing. One day he fell with a collapsing sixth floor and was killed outright. A widow and pregnant, Pauline, faithful to her husband's taste for Nordic symbols, embroidered all of Ibsen on the bibs of the posthumous child, a little girl who was baptised quite simply: Sea Lady.

Pauline likes to think that her daughter has the loveliest tawny hair. In truth, it's carrot-coloured. Which nevertheless does not prevent old Rosalba, her aunt, adoring her and always when she wants to please her clients almost unthinkingly predicting that they'll marry a redhead.

A strange weakness for a fortune-teller, but which isn't surprising once one knows that

1 Halvard Solness, the title character of Ibsen's *The Master Builder* (1892).

83

she did not recognise the resuscitated Myrto-Myrta, Yolande, arriving to consult her. All that spoke was the jealousy which the former flea trainer has always harboured against women. She hates the mysterious, cold and fatal beauty and never misses a chance to say horrible things about her as if after all these years she's still intent on avenging her dear little menagerie, assassinated to the cry of picky pop.

Yolande has seen Pauline again, who also suspected nothing, in Berlin, where she lives with Sea Lady since her remarriage to a very famous facial surgeon.

III

The broderie anglaise bedspread.—The horned hat.—The mask with metal teeth.—Yolande softens.—Weeps over Vagualame.—Vagualame is not fooled.—The germination time is passed, there will be no miracle of a black iris.—Yolande, fatal but sensible, seizes on the word iris.—The iris of irises shines in her eyes.—The fakir's wife, ill-fated star.—What Vagualame sees in the light of memory.—What scarlet star burst, the day before yesterday, in his mouth?—Memories of the skyscraper sanatorium.—The goitrous woman's heart.—Turks in a great hurry to become westerners, instead of feeding their gramophone with the latest negro or New Yorker novelties, stuff it with old couplets from the Parisian suburbs.—The exile clings to one of these tunes which revitalises him, between a shirt shop where everything is pink and a hatmaker who only sells caps, a song-writing mill.—Then, out of the meadow grass, comes the crazy circle of the girls selling mimosa in the cities, along the metro lines.—The Turks' disc, alas, can only make a nasal reproduction of what were the real songs coming from the mouths.—And then, there is no bistro in the sick people's apiary.—The man breaks his thermometer, tears up his temperature records.—Was it worth the bother? To hear the City, Yolande, sighing over him.—A little digression on humano-centricity.—Vagualame calls Yolande the "cheat" and says, not without complaisance, why he called her that.—In a fortnight it will be All Saints Day.

In the centre of the bed,
Revolt is deep.
　　　　(an ancient song).

The inevitable melancholy of him who sleeps alone.—A cursed child, he never wanted to sleep with his mother.—Frightened at this absence of a complex he goes to see a psychoanalyst.—A case of a thirty-year-old woman, of a new-born bat and a tribe of lice.—The psychoanalyst tries with all his might to file him away with the house speciality: the classic Oedipus complex.—So the man resigns himself to being no more than a dusty peninsu-la.—A disappointment for him who loved talking about the ocean, about the river which, running through the middle of the bed, would drown him if he didn't cling to the branches of a ridiculous song.—Vagualame humming it brings upon himself the rage of Yolande.—Yolande chases him away, threatens him.

Having told her story Yolande asks Mr Vagualame if he wants to see the apartment bull and the rat that weighs fifty kilos, both phenomena and in different ways no less extraordinary than the fakir, or whether he would rather come to admire the broderie anglaise bedspread, worked on and presented by the Prince of Wales.

Mr Vagualame opts for the bedspread and Yolande leads him to her bedroom. But she is specific:

"We'll go anyway, in a while, to pay a visit to my dear little monsters. Otherwise, they'll be jealous of the fakir. And then you'll see me wearing my horned hat and my mask with metal teeth, for I stick with the picky pop habit and each evening, before I go to sleep, I throw myself on the bull to pierce his flesh, at least a little, and I nibble at the rat. But here we are at my private quarters. Look at this needlework and admire the skill of the English Crown Prince as it deserves. A real little fairy land, isn't it? Have you looked carefully at it? Then let's sit down. Vagualame, I'm interested in you. Old Rosalba knows how to make people talk, and I know how to make old Rosalba talk. I understand your sadness all the better as I too am sensitive. I've already wept over you...

"Wept over you... wept over you..."

Thus was the sombre porcelain of midnight cleft twelve times by the clock's chimes. But as the clock which hammers insomnia and also the simple delicate watch finally become silent will not Yolande stop shaking the tree of tears? From the hysterical branches the watery fruits fall, to splatter on the ground. Another silence. Yolande will tire herself. And another one. It's the last. Mr Vagualame rubs his hands together. The picky pop, rat-nibble, pierce-bull has not managed to invent a lasting torture for him. Better than that, here she is on the receiving end of a game which she intended as a torment for another. Like birdlime, her velvet dress treacherously sticks her to her chair, a prisoner in her own skin. Behind the bars of her collarbones, the shiver of a captive bird throws itself in exasperation against the skeleton's cage. Already the hairnet of nerves, the proud muscle tissues are no more than a slave's net, an inexorable powerful camisole, somewhere between leather and flesh.

Her mouth, a nest without hope. The sentence which her tongue has been incubating will release no more than a loose wing into the heavens but which drops back, a flabby flock, smelling of burnt rubber, like children's toy balloons when their indigo, green or red roundness crashes into the ceiling.

This balloon keeps on melting.

Then Mr Vagualame speaks:

"Now then, fakir's wife, you're sowing syllables to reap stars, but there is no bouquet of stars blossoming above our heads. On the other hand, a pool of false mystery is watering the fake woollen lawn beneath our feet. By the way, it should be said, my dear, that noblesse oblige, and if you had done things properly you would at least have installed a field in the bedroom for your pet bull. Now, I don't see any sign of greenery amongst the pointless orient of your rug. And anyway it's too late for germination now. So don't expect one of those black iris miracles to gush forth, those black irises with which you boasted just now of being so often compared…"

No doubt Mr Vagualame would have continued speaking for a very long time if Yolande had not picked up on the word iris…

"Iris, iris," she exclaims. "My answer to the cascade of your evil inspiration, Vagualame, is an iris. You would have loved me to be swallowed up by an ocean of vinegar. My eloquence has drowned yours. I can shout louder than a madman. That's why I'm a sensible woman. And a fatal one too. That's a fine slogan: '*Fatal but sensible!*' So have you forgotten that Myrto-Myrta herself shouted: 'Fire' at her execution at Vincennes? So she who is still going, her unbelievable destiny a challenge to death, Yolande, my dear, doesn't give a damn for your evil intentions. You thought she was caught up in her tears. You wanted to niggle her, but ingratitude, that chewing gum of dynamite, in the coffer of your eloquence like Papa Demosthenes' pebbles,[1] could well help your kneading machine of a tongue to make the acquaintance of a nice little explosion. Body and soul, you would be no more than a piece of lace ready to be pinned as a decoration around the embroideries of the Prince of Wales. You refused the black iris, but what if one, blood-coloured and fabulously shaped and lustrous, were to spring from your breast...?"

When he climbed into his seat, Yolande's father, after cracking his whip, never failed to state: "A man's home is his castle." His daugh-

---

1 The Greek orator Demosthenes was said to treat his speech impediment by talking with pebbles in his mouth.

ter well knows that the words pronounced in her home belong to her, as do also whilst they are there any visitors and, for their whole existence into eternity, the fakir, the bull, the rat and those flowers on the rug paid for in hard cash. So why would she refuse to endow with crimson iridescence the transparent ivory of her vowels, as submissive to the voice on its framework of consonants as a glasspaper fan set with cloves is to the flick of a wrist. Iris. Vagualame remembers enough Latin to know that this word is full of anger. But the ire of irises blazes elsewhere than deep in their corollas. You have to reckon too with the ire of the irises between Yolande's eyelashes. Her eyes, more or less colourless, have lit up with a fire which is certainly not one of joy. Vagualame is looking into two drops of pale azure, a look which disdains the imminent conflagration, doubtlessly no less fireproof than a sky on the fourteenth of July, but which nevertheless would not be able to serve as a frontier river between him and she who dragged him from the fog that afternoon in the rue des Paupières-Rouges.

Yolande is no longer the simple survivor of Myrto-Myrta, the paradoxical but still humane resuscitated woman whose bloodless shoulders and breast bloomed forth, a marble siren, from the cascades of spangled black tulle. Yolande, a fiery sun, rips apart and hollows out the night, and Vagualame finds the ruins and wreckage of his past. Yolande could deservedly be called Memory. See, Vagualame, the dried grass of minutes, the burnt savannahs of desire and above all those great trees, too often licked by fire's tongues, the dreams that your pride built with its own hands. A scorched, sooty landscape yet still alive like wood and flesh after a burn. And since a blood-coloured iris is needed, remember, the day before yesterday, no later than the day before yesterday, no less surprising than the icy stalactites in grottoes in the middle of summer, from your cold breast burst forth a warm orchid, of a really scarlet colour for a month when everything is colourless. The scarlet star erupts in your mouth. You lean forward with your eyes closed. When you open them you will see a little pool of bloody mud at the bottom of a bowl. See what comes of loving the town's whores who wear necklaces of papier mâché faces. You had been warned, however. There was not a morning, during those interminable days that you spent on the highest floor of the

skyscraper sanatorium, when the man with
the pointed head who served as your carer did
not come to repeat to you… if you wished,
a few months, a year, two years from now…
What promise, in fact, could the unfinished
sentence be implying? A few months, a year,
two years… yes, but on condition of doing
all that was necessary to deserve being cured,
added the Schwester with the red waxy canvas
cheeks. Deserve to be cured? The first time
you wondered what crime you could have
committed. The second, you were beginning
to understand that a whole highland and
curative mystique was sheltering behind that
formula. From then onwards the Schwester
represented a symbolic value, which in addi-
tion was never contradicted by her gestures
any more than by her words. Thus, she put
on her most playful expression to show you
that she wore dentures. She kindly lifted up
her bonnet of starched linen, the coquette, for
she wanted to show you a lovely little bruised
noddle beneath the sparse locks of her yellow
hair. Vagualame, however, is amazed. The
Schwester is not goitrous. Now, on the day
of his arrival, leafing through the periodicals,
he read in an informative review from Zurich
(*Pro Juventute,* July 1922) that *"according to*

the illustrious professor Dr de Quervain[1] of Berne, the successor to the famous Dr Kocher[2], there are three sorts of goitre, of which the first, ordinary goitre, middle-class goitre, if properly worn, gives an air of authority and respectability." Then, since the most deserving of the great-nephews and nieces of William Tell place between their collarbones and their chin the apple which their ancestor hunted with a crossbow, why would this Schwester, as beautiful as the common concept of an edelweiss, wear such a smooth choker that it certainly leaves no room for the smallest nut? As a response the Schwester has only to open the cylinder of starched canvas that serves as her collar and to indicate the long scar that is thus revealed. Cheerfully, paraphrasing the gospels which she is wild about, and allows Vagualame, whom she supposes to be as doubting as Saint Thomas, to touch with his finger the furrow in her flesh, from which fate would have it that there springs a globule which has, beneath the skin, as decorative an effect as the paperweight on a mantelpiece

---

1 Fritz de Quervain (1868-1940) was a Swiss surgeon and leading authority on thyroid disease.
2 Emil Theodor Kocher (1841-1917) was a Swiss physician and medical researcher who received the 1909 Nobel Prize in Physiology or Medicine for his work in the physiology, pathology and surgery of the thyroid.

with a view of the Chillon castle.

She, a goitrous woman, has through a federal spirit of renunciation, sacrificed the quasi-divine part of herself, and it is her story, totally her story, and nothing but her story which inspired the Helvetian response to *Heart of a French Woman,* for finally Vagualame has guessed that this Schwester is none other than the heroine of *Heart of a Goitrous Woman,* the great work of the famous novelist of Vaud[1] who extols with an honourable lyricism the beefy, chubby, ruddy, homely, Swissy courage of the mountain women who, firmly on their feet, never risk being blown away even when the foehn, that wind of madness, arises from the plains to the south…

Thus, there was once a young girl who lived with her family in a pretty wooden chalet. She would sing *My beautiful pine tree,* pick flowers which she arranged in bouquets and every Sunday go to church in the valley wearing a dress of St. Gallen embroidery, whose delicate collar spread below a suburban goitre which promised much and did not fail to deliver.

An octogenarian poet, a Romansh speaker, blind and semi-paralysed, nevertheless found enough strength in his old body to go on foot from his mountains to those of canton Uri,

1 A Swiss canton.

where the exquisite creature lived, so much did he long before he died to caress this wonderful excrescence with his aged fingers, in order to praise more eloquently this object of conversations, from the plain to the glacier, since a certain photograph had appeared on the front page of an illustrated weekly newspaper in Lucerne above the following words:

> *Minerva was not born from the head of*
> *Jupiter,*
> *But from the neck of Venus.*

Some time afterwards a panel in Berne, charged with identifying a candidate for an international beauty contest to take place in Hollywood, could not do otherwise than recognise in our goitrous girl the most perfect of the country's beauties and certainly, she would not have denied herself this glorious duty if she had not, on the very eve of her election, given her hand to a Tyrolean yodeller who had returned from his military service to his home meadows, with his complexion fresh and no less innocent than that of a musical box dancing figure, for he had been protected from all temptation by the purifying water-lily soup about whose effects Madame de Rosalba, that expert in all things of love and war, had already previously boasted about to Vagualame.

The wedding took place one 1st of August, a national holiday. With her black dress which, according to custom, would come in useful for her period of mourning when God took her husband back to Him, with the white tulle veil, the bouquet of alpine roses in her hands and the goitre gently bobbing at the opening of her bodice, the sweet fiancée looked lovely. Intoxicated with love and alcohol-free wine she nevertheless faithfully followed tradition, going at the end of the day with her family members up to a mountain top to light fires. But the young husband, carried away by happiness, gave out such a resounding layee-od-layee-loodl-oh that he burst a vein in his neck.

Back in the family's chalet the virgin widow decides that in future she will live a life of self-sacrifice, refuse to cooperate with journalists, forbid the local Homers to compose their patois odysseys to the glory of her charms and swear to devote herself unceasingly to those in distress. Providence, listening to her, will soon fulfil her wishes, for at the end of the following winter when she and her family members return from church one Sunday, they find their house has been carried away by an avalanche. The now homeless former inhabitants of the chalet still sing: *My beautiful pine tree,* but it doesn't sound the same. Take courage, brave people. The melancholy is in your voices, but retain your humility in the face of these trials, do not rebel, do not lose confidence, for salvation is coming to you from someone powerful. The wife of the President of the Confederation has never succeeded in getting anything to grow on her epiglottis. Not even a segment of an Adam's apple. Now who could wish more strongly or more sincerely than her for the external signs of honourability, of respectability? For a lady who knows her authors, the sentence of the illustrious professor Dr de Quervain is like a knife twisting in the wound. In Neuchâtel, Fribourg, Zurich, Lucerne, Lausanne, everywhere, in the valleys, on the peaks, she is laughed at. In Berne, they whisper and the bears in the ditches cock a snook when they see her pass by with her neck so scandalously narrow. All through one summer she drank water from the streams, wells and brooks of a valley renowned for its physically and mentally handicapped people, for she would have been happy to have a cretinous goitre if a middle-class one was not available. No doubt she could be accused of demagoguery, but one should at least recognise that she did her best. Alas! It was failure upon failure. Her husband was even talking of casting her aside when, reading by chance about an American millionairess, the victim of an accident which had left her with the external part of an ear missing, had had the bright idea of offering a handsome sum to a poor woman in return for one of her ears, the Swiss Confederation President's wife smiled and clapped her hands: "Eureka, eureka!" A small newspaper announcement: "Goitrous woman sought." A thousand applied. The virgin widow hit the jackpot. Local anaesthetic. A long incision. The kernel comes out of the fruit. Minerva from the neck of Venus. A few stitches. The story of her heroic self-denial will be written until her death on the flesh of her neck in letters made by the scarring. But she must go ahead, abandon the most precious part of her flesh. Sobbing, despite the pride of knowing the laceration is the most poignant symbol of her sacrifice. It is true that the President's wife has some lovely words to calm this pain. Come now, my girl, cheer up, William Tell couldn't have done better. Thanks to you, the chalet will be rebuilt. And with what comforts, what luxury, even in the WCs where rolls of paper are fixed to musical boxes in such a way that, with a clever linking of the useful to the pleasant, the person who pulls the first of the leaves to detach it from the others fixed to it by a perforation, has the nice surprise of suddenly hearing: *The mountain people are here.*

Later, when her younger brothers and sisters are settled, the virgin widow will devote herself to the sick. And why would she refrain from repeating to those whom she will eventually care for that all cures have to be deserved? You have to be a Vagualame to construct so many nasty quibbles. Instead of allowing himself to be moved he tenses up and goes so far as to invent a sort of magic against the goitre-less Schwester. Too clumsy to make a wax figure to stick pins into, he turns to peonies, tulips, whichever red flowers are tough enough not to lose their colour at this altitude and, as if he were attacking the Schwester herself, he martyrises the chubby vermilion of the insipid vegetation.

A symbol of execution for a capital offence, but a symbol denuded of any witchcraft since the goitre-less goitrous woman still comes several times a day, unaffected by evil intentions, to speak the praise of silence, of immobility.

Now, by suffering the virgin linoleum in the foreground, the pine trees in the background and the other Swisseries, against which he finds himself with no protection, for the iron which defended his first dawn from shipwreck has become diluted, melted, evaporated drop by drop, he who would nowhere else resign himself to anything, to anybody, slowly slides, slinks towards submission and, like the other bees in the apiary of the sick, awaits the gramophone's hour when he can amid the confused buzzing choose one of the tunes to intoxicate him like the most essential liquor.

He always leaps upon the disc of his neighbours, a strong-willed Turkish couple whose age is impossible to tell like that of trees, for beneath the adipose Ottoman exterior there beats a youthfulness desperate to become westerners but which a joint pulmonary weakness forces them to stop on the threshold of the cogitating Confederation. Although having very good intentions the couple are still incapable of distinguishing between the specialities of States and their major cities, and, for example, have perfumes brought from Naples, find wit in Belgian newspapers, ask the English press for impartial opinions on communism and the soviets and, instead of feeding the gramophone with the latest novelties from New York, stuff it with 1900-style waltzes, each one a feverish February stroller reminiscent, between a shirt shop where everything is pink and a hatmaker who only sells caps, of a song-writing mill where with earphones on his ears and his eyes enthralled by the vivid colours of the wall coverings he would become drunk on the words and the rhythms which, one by one, were prickled by a thousand daggers of jealousy, clouded with a riverbank sadness as soft as a slightly frayed dark blue silk, illuminated by colours more boastful than those of Japanese paper playthings and, still, penetrated by the scent of poor streets, rain, red wine, chip fat and violet-flavoured rice powder.

Then from the Swiss window, from today's opening, the past comes back to life, coming from the meadow grass, the nervous and boring theory of the gypsies who have always sold, and always will sell, mimosa in the cities and along the metro lines. Wearing their most insolent smiles, these girls who for their flower trays choose the least fragile blooms are now collecting the too-mauve end-of-summer meadow saffron.

It turns, it turns, the Turks' disc.

Bohemians, sirens of the streets, you will become mad women in these pastures and already one of your eyes has become a poppy even if the other remains coal.

It turns, it turns, the disc.

The wax platter turning so quickly, the couplets emanating from it, more suffocating than the smoke of brambles burning on the ground, and the slim gipsy girls whose number grows and who suddenly sit down in a circle with their arms raised holding aloft wilting bouquets, and start to turn, turn, turn, each one spinning faster and louder than the discs, faster and louder than the maddest dervishes, for this whirlwind which the earth would not forgive for moving counter to its own motion, for three words and two verses of the refrain, its axis, the man would give the earth and all its inhabitants.

It turns, it turns, the disc.

But it was certainly not with impunity, since autumn was already descending from the mountains, the same grey colour as the scree, and the little cows whose milk is certainly never as good as skin whitener for cream on the vitriol pastries of the poor quarters.

And besides, the gramophones grind away.

Now here is the sixtieth, the last minute of your reign. Time for you to be quiet. Silence, that felted bird, splits, wounds the sky with a long artful furrow.

One rebel, just a single one, but at least one, howls with great scarlet cries.

Everyone is afraid. And you first, the man who frequented the song-writing mills, you should love red. Yes, you should, for goodness' sake. You remember the wild silks you tied around your neck. Hypocrisy. You didn't have the least faith in the colour of your blood. You wrapped yourself in violent purple, but simply against draughts. You spoke of risks and you feared head colds. You claimed to like whores, rogues, their offerings, the ill-famed streets and all that's going to the dogs, but the sight of an open razor made your teeth chatter, and you've been living for months stretched out on a balcony.

With an egoism that only hears the Turks' disc, could you deny that for weeks and weeks nothing has interested you except the sickness, your temperature and the very boredom whose aristocratic usage you took longer to detect than an Eskimo would to learn to ride a bicycle?

A miserable international association of rotting breasts, a tubercular syndicate, a coughing freemasonry with, since the time of the Romantics, skeletal graces, cousins of the pretentious bourgeoise holding out her little finger as she lifts her cup of mocha coffee to her foul lips.

The goitrous woman, for example, likes to see the feverishness and the sparks it causes in the eyes of the sick, like shiny worms on the lawns at night. Deep down, she wishes a little 40° on those whom she exhorts with her "You have to earn a cure", from the same and equally vile inspiration as the *Enrich Yourself* of that fellow Guizot.

Earn your cure, enrich yourself, badly put together.

Breathe with all your soul, all your hope, don't speak, don't move, since even the air, on the highest floor of the skyscraper sanatorium, is given the status of a medication.

And do not leave your chaise-longue, even if your fingers are freezing despite the season which for half a week still is called summer. Forget the supposedly sensual zinc of the bar counters, the way your hands grabbed at it last year, for there is no bistro in the apiary of the sick, not a stretch of wall where a sheaf of saltpetre can spread itself between columns of bottles, not a table whose waxed cloth, like marble, shows its purplish zigzags, its terrifying ribs, its peninsular antics, its white and black jagged outlines against a red background, enough rivers, enough roads to satisfy hopes, dreams. But the spirit which cannot spread its wings in its prison wishes to fly away. But you cannot float in emptiness. You will not reach the ether, so high up. I had told you. And boom! You've crashed into the mountains. Now your wandering eye would like to become a mollusc, an oyster to be scoffed, but no compassionate mouth will drink your tears, this miserable encapsulation of an ocean, out of which love alone would resuscitate the sea and its infinite visions.

Decidedly, you've had enough.

You break your thermometer, tear up your temperature records.

You take the train for Paris. But once there you realise that past, long past, is the time of the feverish February stroller.

To recapitulate: Mme de Rosalba.

The rue des Paupières-Rouges.

At last Yolande, at whose house you've ended up. She's not saying anything, neither are you. You're stretched out on her bed.

She doesn't even grudge you dirtying with your shoes the Prince of Wales' deliciously ochreous work, but as you're slipping, you're going to fall, roll on the carpet, she wraps her stony arm around your body, as if she feared that without being saved by her strength you would be scattered around—all of you, bones, thoughts, muscle shapes, remnants of hope. She wants to be your harness. You dream of a geranium-scented mouth, a heart of blood-sapped petals ripped from some mysterious corolla and flaming with the very fire which is the centre of the earth.

In the eyes of the woman, your neighbour, a red spark gives away their sea-green hypocrisy.

The coachman's daughter, Myrto-Myrta, Yolande, call her what you will, this person of transformations. Vagualame, among other names, deserves especially 'Memory' which you adorned him with as late as today. An ember, in Memory's gaze, lights up like a pinhead and will not be magnified into a forest of tall flames.

She has seized on the word 'iris'.

She has spoken so that from her voice, that bubble of sound, the moment is irised. If it had been a question of begonias, she would have claimed to begoniaise the universe, since everything has to serve her purpose so that she can revel in syllables in the same the way as she was rubbed by the fakir. In other words, Yolande knows life and there is not a creature, plant, mineral, not a nuance, a contact, a dwarf or giant monstrosity, not a scrap of echo, shadow or reflection, of which she has not discovered unexpected possibilities.

She has foreseen all the uses of the world and her three identities, from the mysteries of India to the royal heir to the English throne's taste for needlework, and as in the Épinal images[1] a mysterious machine can make a top hat out of a rabbit, in the same way she would deliberately change everything for her own profit into beauty products, furnishings, decorative whimsies etc.... Such stubborn egoism implies so much faith in existence that not even for five minutes was she surprised at her resurrection and beneath the diversity of aspects and expressions which identified in turn her persona she has never ceased to recognise herself as one and total at the same time. You, Vagualame, should be inspired

1 Épinal images were prints in bright colours popular in France in the 19th century, first published by Jean-Charles Pellerin who was born in Épinal.

by this miraculous vitality to, for example, choose a toothpaste with a good name, a good colour. You would try some, and because to try it is to adopt it, and not wanting to keep putting your charms in doubt you would then smile an irresistible smile. You could propose an alliance with Yolande. She would accept and, with together the fakir, the apartment bull and the rat weighing fifty kilos, you would do some laps of honour. But what's this? You're refusing to speak. Yet you know perfectly well that silence between you is as incomprehensible as a scalped comet. She will not tolerate this baldness. Faithful to the infallible picky-pop method she will sigh over the sighing one:

"Last night I dreamed of you, I wept."

Once again!… The Woman, the City, all of them, they have the same refrain on their lips?

Scorning the tearful nocturne which his sleep, incapable of inventing its own stars, took delight in between yesterday and today, Vagualame thinks that a little rage always enters into the chemical composition of tears, and Yolande, before wakening, had already imagined the morning against her windows and the repeated small crystals so difficult to harass. Vengeance, she had wanted the man's feeling of pity to serve as his prison, but he, like the monkeys in the zoo, always ready to laugh at those walking by whose steps they believe are limited by the bars of their own cage, he has succeeded in turning away the pity which the woman claimed to surround him with.

He bursts out:

"You wept, woman, you dreamed.

"Tears, your tears, tears.

"You love pomp and circumstance. So use it for a presentation.

"Vagualame…

"Tears, dream.

"Tears, an orphanage of navels, a seed bed of spice bread hearts, a deluge of toothless smiles."

All the facets of Lent appear in order to watch the dream, wrapped closely in a jersey patterned with lozenges of fire and ice above their salty hair, leaping from tree to tree so joyfully supple that it is not even possible to imagine there are bones in his body. But the shrikes are getting cross. They pull at the short straw to find out who will seize hold of the incredible acrobat by his foot of flame.

"Fate chooses the oldest woman."
                    (*A well-known song.*)

So these ladies climb up on each other's shoulders and she whom fate chooses, perched at the top of the wobbling pyramid, drags the acrobat off his branch. And then they all jump down to the ground, surround, trample and tear apart the Harlequin of ice and fire. At daybreak, the old women will lament the faded, melted dream.

And yet it was perfectly simple to leave the dance its freedom, on the ocean of leaves. Only its phosphorescence would have lit up, illuminated the greyest of faces and perhaps the draught of air, the shoulder squeezer, infinitely multiplied, in its twilight and shivering power, had become a tempest, the real tempest, coming from no-one knows where, snatching their secrets from the chasms, from the mountain peaks, sweeping the sky above the most mediocre suburbs and, between heaven and earth in its flaming flight shakes its locks of hurricane and surprise upon the foreheads of the inspired.

Now, because of tears, because of the City, because of you, Yolande, and because of anyone who tried to interfere with the dream, the oak trees, the palm trees, and willows and the giant irises have all gone back into the earth. So, Vagualame, dream of the virgin forest as much as you please, but know that of all the plants just one remains, a creeper rolled up somewhere over there, winding itself around a young sleeping girl to protect her from a mysterious current of air. No doubt this is the Redhead predicted by Rosalba, Sea Lady, the niece whom Yolande hates. Her sleep must not be compost to nourish the juicy plants of vulgar desires. She sleeps with a crown of blue-green rhythms and the hour which cradles her is a wave undisturbed by ships or wrecks. No foam will come sadly to embellish her awakening, for with her eyelids closed a thousand thousand tidal waves are guillotining the fish, torpedoes of anguish whose whims electrocute the man, your look-alike Vagualame.

So regret.

And above all regret that lyrical chasm, of which no sounding rod has touched the bottom. You are afraid of seasons and bare hands. You have rejected your youth, all bones and jaws. You wear woollen gloves, and gentle but treacherous algae decorate your hours. You are not very deep, and yet you do not dive into yourself, for your foot, when feeling its way, would not be able to find its footing on the last rock. Besides, why would you want to come back up to the surface, since you collect not pearls but anecdotes of shellfish.

You cling to stories. You embrace words, you love experiencing the slightest palpitation of the facts. You're like a man who would strangle himself just for the joy of feeling the life gasping beneath the skin of his neck.

So, what is the point of the look, the flames or sparks coming from the rubbing together of sounds and colours, if the very mystery does not prove its essential and elusive identity with the fire that warms our dwellings, cooks our food, but must never at the height of dreams end its immaterial dance?

The earthly globe, the men, women, animals, the things that inhabit it are there to tempt weakness. You would not want to die without seeing Venice, Tahiti, the two Americas. When you meet children you try to find words which decide their future. You say: this is a seductive child, this one an obscene child, and in the countryside you stroke the grass as if it were a dog you loved. Yet Nature, as capitalised as you like, with its flora and fauna is as you know well nothing but a dictionary, no doubt a dictionary with surprises where the dream sometimes finds its verb, but a dictionary all the same, and nothing but a dictionary.

So start by despising the letter which is not doubled by the flamboyant spirit.

Fruits, chairs, boats, continents, seas, pools of sunshine, slaps of rain, the degoitred goitrous woman, Mimi Patata and her twins, the Prince of Wales and his embroideries, Rosalba and her predictions, Yolande and the fakir, the apartment bull and the rat, this whole mosaic in which your life itself is just a dot, are worth nothing unless, beyond their frontiers, beyond their usual contours, an echo resuscitates them, changed and better than themselves.

Moreover, you have thus loved the night as your most beautiful, magnificent and single vengeance. At the moment when the star is to be precise finally overturned, because there are no more facts but simply risks, then from the interaction of light and shade the miracle of transubstantiation is born. We are proud that everything becomes purple. And we know the reign of disproportionate things.

But the City and Yolande who, to explain the difficulty of rebirth as day breaks, have shortened to fit their conscience, their aware-ness, the memory of an enthusiasm, even if you were the cause of their tears by only having seen the principle of emotion, you would need a speck in the eye of the fire whose whole must be judged by whoever boasts of a life superior to the everyday.

A poet[1] has imagined two mirrors, one opposite the other with nothing in between, except a gaze with no body, no flesh, so that the notion of the infinite was no longer reduced to words.

Alas, you know only too well, you miserable creature, that your physical presence is an object more difficult than any other to forget, to hide. The part of you which has the miracle of the conjugate mirrors would not be able, despite the most heroic words, to prevent your obsessive individuality sliding between the two reflective surfaces.

So instead of an ecstasy of words it would be an infinitely repeated Narcissism. One head, two heads, three heads, four, five, fifty, a hundred, five hundred, a thousand, a hundred thousand heads. But how would eyes, which still remember the palace of mirages of the Thursdays of childhood, be dazzled, when a simple piece of green paper with its reflected cut-out shapes created an inextricable forest?

1 Francis Picabia, 1879-1953, a French avant-garde painter, poet and typographer.

It's your fault, you over-educated heart.

Better than yourself, any old fairy lantern would light up those galas which you still wish to give to yourself. Because the stars no longer mix their light with your blood, a dull river waters that flesh, your flesh. Your hair has lost its wild insolence ad your eyes no longer hope ever to shine.

You would like to confess but you have no crimes.

Yolande and you remain facing each other, with no more to say to each other than china dogs.

Your ears are rococo weights.

Not a moment of you which deserves resurrection, and it was quite fair that this day started with a dawn of tin, and that no face gushed over or leaned over either one or the other of your awakenings. You know it, Vagualame, and you know that the tears of those like you are not so valuable that one must stubbornly honour you for them. So, once and for all, reject this lyrical responsibility, but note that you know no-one of your kind who is worth even a drop of salty water. So the other poet[1] was right when he cried: "We must desensitise the universe".

1 Paul Éluard 1895-1952, a French poet and one of the founders of the Surrealist movement.

Despite square hands, badly attached legs, fatness and the sickening little thoughts that swell inside them, and the bourgeois goitres which they carry for real and figuratively, all men, in books, theatres, museums, seek only their own portrait. Thus all French women have read *Coeur de Française*[1]. The same principle applies to Greek statuary, to the success of Phidias and Co.

Now, if one hooks up reality's little bell, you, Vagualame, you will say very judiciously that between a marble of the best period, sent directly from the Acropolis, and a young pimp with bare torso and limbs and wearing just, between the thighs and the navel, small pink and white cotton shorts, sunning himself in the summer on the plage des Catalans[2] in Marseille, it's the pimp who wins. In the same way, the large four-legged wet-nurses with wings, known by the name of sphinxes, have for a long time made you think it is dishonest to tear from phantoms the airiest of their attributes in order to use them to decorate creatures which two heavy pairs of feet would fix to the ground.

---

1 'The Heart of a French Woman' by Arthur Bernède (1871-1937).
2 'Beach of the Catalans'.

For the rest, if you despise these four-legged creatures, it's because you have thousands and thousands of feet to carry you. You move so quickly that you have no time to stop for anything, for an idea. Not even unfaithful, since we don't know of you having any relationship, but always drawn this way and that. And the endless dream of a great mysterious underground force which you hope will one day throw you far away beyond horizon and habit to where it is time for the sun of sulphur and love to burst forth.

This sun is the egg from which the flame bird will be hatched. But which the crafty bird catchers will never try to tame. But enough of the heart-breaking fable of Psyche who lost love through having wanted to experience it. Besides, Vagualame, you only have to look at your fingers. Far too rough for you to dare offering them as a perch for the intangible dove. Moreover, what does it matter if the bird is an intangible dove, a bearded skylark, a musical triangle, provided with feathers as cleverly worked as those adorning Mercury's mythological hat, and even if it was an elephantine eagle, green goose or a vulgar plucked vulture, it deserves a name at least as equal in beauty to that of the cheetah. But above all, Vagualame, never call it either God or the devil, for the humans' sky would be too narrow for its spreading wings, and no-one would be able to imagine a hell vast enough for the flames which crown it.

How can the creature whose dream was brushed by this violent sweetness which is neither white nor black, nor blue, nor red, but white and black, and blue and red, dare, on awakening, to have recognised in it the caress of one palm and not another, the smile of a certain mouth? But the eyes are nonetheless continuing to take for tears, their tears, dawn's blinding dew.

Yolande, the City, all of you who wanted to light up with a name the tender hour which did not have one, Vagualame anoints you cheats.

YOLANDE—Me, a cheat? Why?

VAGUALAME—A cheat because you play heads or tails.

YOLANDE—Heads or tails?

VAGUALAME—Yes, heads or tails and tails or heads and heads or heads and tails or tails. You weep, you dream, you weep, but what is the point of giving a human form to this dampness?

During your childhood, when an incomprehensible sun shone behind the curtain of rain, your coachman father would say: "Look, there's the devil who beats his wife". Today, although there are no conjugal ties between us, you would like to avenge your sex, beat the man. Your timing was not well chosen. For days and days there has not been the slightest paradoxical storm, or rainbow ring on the fidgety fingers of the minutes. It's autumn, Yolande, a horrible season. In the city of flesh the zinc of my obsessive temptation on the top floor of the skyscraper sanatorium will no longer flow, that lyrical, cold and supposedly sensual tenderness in the hands of my bore-dom. On the 15 October over there in the south it is a reddish hypocrisy, and my feet will no longer be able to find the fragile path of the heatwaves between the fire falling from the sky and the shade softer than a violet grape. Broken is the thread that the gaze could not detect and that nevertheless would follow the steps, mistress of the blinding alternance and without ever the slightest vertigo at the deep chasm of light, to the right, nor at that coolness to the left, hollowing the paving of the earthly projection of the high walls rising to the azure heights…

And there is Vagualame who once again has forgotten Yolande while he remembers a city by the water which has never claimed to weep or to dream of anyone, the very opposite of a rue des Paupières-Rouges where one meets a woman with a fakir and picky-pop. Walking, lost in the garden of heavy peonies, a young girl was passing by, so lightly that her feet were like the leaves of a plant unattached by any root to the ground, and from her silhouette rose a shadow, ascended to the clouds where to his sweetest joy the man saw the lion, the wolf, the gazelle galloping. But a transparent fawn will always find it difficult to exist, and whilst the sphinxes and still scraping at the sand of the oldest deserts, one evening great carnivores with terrifying names started crunching, and all night went on crunching, the bones of animals with beige coats and distant gazes.

And now the espadrilles-wearing people are silent, they who tossed, like lassos to seize the azure, the couplets whose nasal caricature the Turks offered at the hour of the gramophones.

But don't think for a minute about leaving for the port, the capital of the rogues you called robin redbreasts because of the scarves that you like, Vagualame, but which they, the muscular blackguards, tie around their necks just for the pleasure of it. A fortnight from now it will be All Saints' Day, in Marseille as elsewhere. Wreaths will be thrown into the sea. A fake Neapolitan will not warm himself by eating flames and the girls' voices will be muffled, their eyes evil, for the rain is already piercing the frayed silk of their bodices, over-whelming the curve of their backs, their legs ill-protected and their feet broken and sway-ing in poor shoes with over-high heels.

The most perfidious of seasons is falling upon the entire universe. Vagualame, you don't know where to go and yet you must go. What, at this time, does your presence signify with the woman and her fakir? Of course, you've no wish to make love with this piece of ice.

So, you must take your courage in both hands, resume the conversation, say goodbye…

And then…

And then, it will be oasis, sleep.

But what's this?

Your teeth are chattering, you're shivering and with a distant gaze, although Yolande is not three metres in front of you, suddenly you're starting to sing softly:

In the centre of the bed,
The river is deep.

You keep repeating it until your litany is cut off by sniggering, your own sniggering.

Then a speech starts, more a soliloquy, for once again you're speaking for yourself, which the professionally seductive pride of a former dancer could very well be exasperated by. It is true that you yourself reminded her of it. *Noblesse oblige.* So the friend of the Prince of Wales will be able to hold herself back. Her fingers might well drum on the arms of the chair, and despite them she will let you chatter nevertheless. And you will go for it:

I, Vagualame, I must go home to bed. Alone. At night, as a child, when I went to sleep I would always have next to me a teddy bear and a small locomotive. I was in love with both of them, certainly more in love than my father was with Mummy Bijou, as recalled by old Rosalba this afternoon with an enthusiasm as misplaced as anachronistic, since she, now deceased, who gave birth to me, was during her life too unconcerned about charming her son for any sensuality to be awakened. A sniffly baby, from the age of ten months I preferred the chamber maid to her, a certain Lucie whose perfume smelled of carnations.

For the child of French bourgeois parents, a mother is piece of furniture, in the same way as the Henri II dresser, the Pleyel[1] in the living room or the parents' large imitation Louis XVI bed.

A little more naïve no doubt than the others and, with hindsight, frightened by my puerile frigidity, once I reached the age of manhood I went to see a psychoanalyst.

He started with questions:

"Where have come from?"

"From seeing a woman."

"Her age?"

"Twenty-nine."

"Yours?"

"Twenty-six."

"Perfect. The woman you went to see was older than you. First point. Did you experience any emotion in her presence? And of what sort, of what intensity?"

"A new-born bat, which had fallen from I don't know where, was flattened on the ground of the terrace where we were. An adult bat doesn't really excite me. But a new-born,

---

1 A make of upright piano.

with its poor soft flesh, cold, mauve, exposed and especially that one, with its wings torn, its neck broken, its breast like marmalade…"

"Very good, very good. Which animal do you dislike above all others?"

"The louse."

"Better and better. Do you have living brothers or sisters?"

"I had a brother. He is dead. I still have two living sisters."

"Which of the three do you prefer?"

"My sisters."

"Are they older than you?"

"No, my brother was the eldest."

"Then you must be mistaken, Monsieur. Or rather, you don't dare to say what you think. The resistance phenomenon. A phenomenon well known to psychoanalysts. A last question, please. Would you be afraid of going blind?"

"More than anything in the world."

"Everything is clear, very simply. We are experiencing a banal, classic case of the Oedipus complex. You went to see a woman older than you, the mother. Without the slightest compassion for the baby bat which killed itself falling from its nest, the poor thing, instead of feeling for it on the contrary you felt nothing but disgust, distaste, and you hate inoffensive lice but which are by defi-nition parasites, so symbols of those smaller than you, those yet to be born and who you were afraid would arrive and steal from you the maternal affection which you thought was owed to you. You're shaking your head? You won't admit it and you would like to delude others as you delude yourself, unconsciously certainly, I admit, when you claim to have preferred and still to prefer your elder brother to your younger sisters. But let us proceed to analysis. I'll take a pencil and paper and sit behind you. Then, according to the method which you are well aware of, speak, describe without hesitation whatever comes into your head. Just a second please. Forget I'm here. I'm listening."

"No use doctor. I've never been able to speak to someone who's not in my field of vision, even of something I've prepared. The subconscious is not the ostrich's granddaugh-ter. A presence would perhaps drag out its se-cret. An ambush, never. Would you go cheer-fully at night into a deserted ill-famed street if you were sure that behind the fence of the waste land were unseen scoundrels watching you passing by? If the majority of men take pleasure in thinking about suicide very few submit to it, but none allow themselves to be murdered. So, doctor, I avoid those dead-end streets where I would be forced by a knife at my neck to empty my bag. And then after all, why don't we put our cards on the table? I know what I'm doing, and that I'm suffering not from the classic Oedipus complex, but from the anti-Oedipus simplex. Deep down in my heart, between the paving slabs of the back courtyard, not even enough earth for the grass of obsession. That's why I don't know how to pass the time. I have never desired my mother. I have just lifted the skirts of a kitchen girl, in the country, when I was four years old. Well, cursed be the man who didn't want to sleep with his mother. Those suffering from the Oedipus complex are not the sick ones since they are pretty much the totality. On the other hand, poor isolated fellow, suffering from the anti-Oedipus simplex I could, to paraphrase Saint Theresa, howl to the four winds that I'm suffering from not suffering.

"But as for the resistance phenomenon, no doubt dear to Mr de la Palice,[1] I have lied, not about my brothers and sisters, but concerning the lice, for to be frank I adore these delicious little creatures. If I don't give them a

1 Jacques de la Palice (1470-1525), a French nobleman and military officer.

little goodnight in their hairy bushes, I dream all night that their underground nephews, termites, alongside this solitary body that no sensual pleasure has made invulnerable, go about digging their gallery along my legs, my trunk, my arms, my neck. And I collapse, a peninsula of dust upon the pale ocean of the sheets.

"Peninsula.

"You can still go with your phallic symbol, but as everything, as it diffuses, becomes confused, for example pantheism, becoming in the end all one, with atheism, thus the pansexual interpretation of creatures puts them all into the same sac, a carefully crafted puerile uniform made of scrotum skin which crushes the man's sexual organ, whilst that of the woman is sewn with small stitches of the very thread that holds together the parts of the costume. In the end this subject does not seem to be very erotic, equally not erogenic or erophilic, and certainly with less subtle veins and grains than the marble of the Third Republic's statues.

"Now, doctor, I'm asking you into what sort of rotten globule will the revolutionary spirit, the liberating strength of a science which you claim to serve but which in reality you make use of, into what sort of rotten globule will it be metamorphosed by your hands, of which one is laziness and the other imbecility? And why must it be that a dwarf claims to seize the lofty words, believes himself taller than they are?"

"Sir," the doctor interrupts, "Science's worth is only in its application. So if you dislike my manner, continue to do without psychoanalysis. Wallow in your complexes until the day when…"

"What? Threats? But if I did have complexes they would be too precious for me to ever accept their removal. The worthiest among men do not have to nurture their inferior brothers with their own vows, their own substance. And what would you do, psychoanalyst, with what you'd taken from me? You must be full to bursting with all the mediocre secrets extorted from your clients. A thief, like the others who don't know what to do with their spoils, always the same trash, the same concealment in the shadow of the temple from which the man named Jesus chased away the moneylenders. But you would need to start by destroying the temple itself, that palace of torture which masochist humanity took centuries and centuries to construct for itself. Dynamite was unknown, you'll cry, at the time of the Nazarene. A fine excuse. The truth, men, the truth, us, the truth, me, the truth is that there is not enough phosphorus, not enough scarlet rage in the blood of our hearts. Hands too small (look, I'm offering you twice five phalluses, psychoanalyst), my hands which I would have liked to be palms of light, their ten fingers, their double anaemic swellings did not even try to tear up the pasteboard of the fake ramparts surrounding me. I live in a cage, like my little friends, a captive and victim too often proud of the deceptive individualism which sets one creature against another to the pointless joy of the psychologists, the mundane novelists, and that multifarious breed the lovers of gossip and tittle-tattle. Salvation is nowhere, and will be nowhere, as long as people believe it's for some and not for others. The wise old man of Vienna who showed the naked silhouettes which were hidden, to the direst confusion, by the complicated drapery of ancestral and futile phantoms, his admirable words will have no effective value until the day when the crowd, the mob, the rabble, as you say, having stripped them of the snobs and the ribald theory of the conservative rationalists who mimic audacity, this crowd, this mob, this rabble will turn out to be aggressive enough, inexorable enough to use the words towards and against everyone, for even knowledge is got with blood and he who wishes to acquire it must, after denouncing myths such as that of education for all and a thousand others of the same sort, remove the possibility of doing harm from those who, having dispensed fake benefits, only wished to appear to teach in order to better conceal the most essential of liberating hypotheses.

"So stop wrapping children in false humility or do not be surprised that, as adults, they wish to return to the maternal bosom, and to forget the world where everything is compulsion."

See, Vagualame, peninsula of dust because:

> *In the centre of the bed*
> *The river is deep.*

The River?

He who loved to speak of the ocean, now he's very modest. Because of his vanity, his phraseology, his previous metaphors were no doubt in danger of becoming imprecise and even incomprehensible. But if the beautiful spirit of the Café du Commerce, in any town of our dear France which has a firm mind and knows what's what, could claim that our hero well deserved to be called Vagualame, the not-beautiful spirit of the Café of no-Commerce , in any small town of an ideal country, which doesn't have a firm mind and doesn't know what's what, will reply that, in this chaos there was a frankness in spades and which was worth more than any perfectly straight lie and which moreover will not prevent the not-beautiful spirit deploring the fact that this diver into the deepest good intentions should have wanted the river to swallow him up.

Vagualame, you peninsula of dust dreaming at the top of your voice, now awake, it's a pity that Yolande, this piece of cold vanity, can hear you shouting your head off like that, that a little draught of air would spread to the four corners of the heavens and a pool would drown the small pile of cinders that you are. Suddenly you are moved by an incomprehensible indulgence for your hands which are so white and would make a beautiful double water lily. Nevertheless, when one drowns one tries to embrace something as one passes by. Vagualame clings to a song, the first he ever heard, the one with which during his earliest months he was cradled by his wet nurse, a Breton woman at whose breast this unnatural child, lacking instinct, did not even know how to feed spontaneously.

But a fig for the past.

These are the words howled by our hero, to a rather doubtful tune:

> *Everyone there stinks*
> *Smells of carrion*
> *There's only my sweet Jesus*
> *Who smells of eau de Cologne*
> *Yum yum yum my sweet saviour*
> *Who has the good smell.*

And there you go, it's too much.

The insolence of this couplet would make Yolande hopping mad if, as a grand lady, she did not know how to keep herself in check.

"When I was little, monsieur, I would often ask what sort of animal was the boor. If I had met you I would not have needed to repeat that question. That said, I think we have seen enough of each other. I have nothing further to say to you. How could I have, a few minutes ago, confided the secret of my life in you? You are of evil character and someone who sings such imbecilities should inspire great fear. *Yum, yum, yum my sweet saviour.* I'll give you some yum and some yum, the real ones you'll see, when I get the fifty-kilo rat to nibble at you. This rodent and the apartment bull will make short work of finishing off Vagualame's carcass. Your salvation is Patata. She knows you're with me. I wish she'd go to the devil. Let her leave quickly for India and buy herself such a good time there with the Maharajah's thirty pairs of twins that she won't want to come back. So, watch out for your skin. Come on, be off, goodnight."

"Goodnight madame."

"Ah, if you had understood me just now, I was ready to love you. My unearthly beauty, what a fuss! It's not for those of this world."

"Adieu madame."

"Adieu monsieur, and bon voyage."

"Actually, since you're speaking of a journey, I was intending to fulfil Rosalba's predictions and get to know the Redhead, your niece, Sea Lady, who you told me is in Berlin?"

"Do it, monsieur. We will meet again there, for I've agreed to present my fakir at the Wintergarten. The Germans love variety shows. They're paying me a crazy price. I shall be idolised, very powerful. Do it, monsieur, but it will be war. Watch out for yourself."

IV

Vagualame in Berlin.—Seeking Sea Lady, whose stepfather he has not forgotten is a specialist in facial surgery.—At the patcher-up of faces, Herr Dr Herzog.—The mother of Sea Lady, Frau Dr Herzog, with her face half repaired, is an advertisement for her husband.—Sea Lady has had a strange operation.—The sexual institute of Dr Optimus Cerf-Mayer.—Where we meet the brother of the heroine with the goitrous heart, a Swiss pervert.— An abnormal adolescent in canton Vaud.—The fetishism of butter-coloured gloves.—Balzac and Mme Hanska, at Neuchatel.—Ovaries and otaries.—Another song.—Sea Lady is in love with and loved by an American woman, Miss Patre, forename Cleo.—What do you say to that, Papa Ibsen?—Emma Psychology.—She's wearing stockings of the same blue as Mme Hanska, Hanska, the beautiful Polish woman.—In the depths of the fjords, in the haunted house.—Byron and his lovers.—The Museum of the Sexual Institute.—An eonism séance.—A procession of mannequins.—

Yolande's arrival.—What the Swissy calls a schön lokal.—The gaze of a pretty Berlin girl.—Cards on the table.—Vagualame is René Crevel.—During Yolande's absence, the apartment bull and the rat weighing fifty kilos have disembowelled and gnawed the fakir.—Death of Yolande.—I refuse to adopt a documentary tone to speak about Berlin, the capital of Prussia and of purity.—There is no oasis.—Gulf Stream of the spiritual map of the world.—Swim on your back.

In Berlin.

As he had not forgotten that the stepfather of Sea Lady, the stepbrother of Yolande unbeknownst to her, was a specialist in facial surgery, Vagualame checked the telephone directory for the names of qualified male stylists who cut, carve, trim your skin with the same and equally joyful carefree manner as if it were a question of the softest felt, two creases on each temple, folds and overcast stitches under the chin and a small turn-up for the noses of the beautiful Prussian ladies who, from seeing the Lancret paintings in the cold rooms and corridors of the Sans-Souci Palace, dream of Pompadour-style little faces and the graces of that Barbarina whose very name is a symbol, for the eighteenth-century Frenchman, a great traveller, in order to hide ideas which the customs officers of the time would not allow past, would hide in his luggage a batch of completely frivolous paintings, silks and trinkets and especially a thousand baubles which he pinned in the North-East of Europe, on that beautiful exterior which, without being overly metaphorical, could well represent a large bosom with big firm breasts, paradoxical amongst the rococo style of the finery whose excesses, on the contrary, rendered even more beautiful that barbarity, so beautiful that it was just called Barbarina, and could only be called Barbarina, the dancer, a butterfly of tulle and flame, a she-devil spinning on her points and unbelievable among the girls with big feet, the real figure of Barbarity, in the magnificent and icy solitude of the heathlands where the most basic fruits need a hothouse, and so troubling that old Frederick when he wanted to pay her the homage of his virility, but needing caution, could in the end only offer her a cup of tea.

The craze for believing in the possibility of better times, although lecturers and journalists persist in speaking of the Despair and the sickness of this century, allows one hundred and forty practitioners, in a single European capital, to live, or to have reasons for hoping to live, off patching up anatomies and expressions.

Working through in alphabetical order had already taken up a week of Vagualame's time when, arriving at the letter H, he collected information on the Privatdozent[1] Karl Herzog which gave him to believe that he had at last found his man. So he went off to ask him if his rather snout-like nose could be changed into one in the style of those of the great Condé family.

"Basic stuff," came the reply. "Local anaesthetic. We open up, we fill with paraffin and after shaping we sew up. The patient just has to say what he wants, and according to his choice, his nose will become hooked like a Baltic baron's, aquiline, bourbon-style, or straight like a Greek's, and moreover without risking losing any of his olfactory faculties…"

In order to get the face mender to leave behind the generalities and go along the path of confidences, Vagualame suddenly pretended to hesitate, to become worried to know if this redemption through iron and wax did not at all risk spoiling for him, even a little, his looks,

1 An unsalaried university lecturer or teacher in a German-speaking country remunerated directly by students' fees.

and if, for example, Dr Herzog would dare do such an operation on one of his family members, or if, what would be really convincing, he had already dared to and succeeded.

The Privatdozent fell right into the trap and sent for Frau Dr Herzog herself, since he had practised his craft on the face of his own wife.

In profile, seen from the right, the Frau Dr looked twenty years old. From the left, she looked fifty. Full face, half-virginal, half-wrinkled; you would think a vertical line passed down the middle of her forehead, her nose, her lips, her chin, to separate youthfulness and wrinkliness with a line no less ideal but equally as clear as the equator between the two hemispheres of our globe. Now, what would a traveller or a navigator in the tropics say if the invisible circle with which the geographers have encircled the earth indicated two portions still more or less equal in weight, heat, mass and matter, but looking so unlike each other that one appeared scorched by fires, the sirocco, the fevers and torments of the evenings, whilst the other, which touches it, comes just before it, sticks to it without the slightest transition, remains as fresh as the dawning of the day?

The paradoxical Frau Dr, with fifty per cent of her face patched up, serves as living proof: Before. After. And besides she has nothing to complain about an operation that has made her famous, since all the expressionist painters have wanted to paint her portrait. A philosopher of the University of Jena, the author of a learned work on asymmetry and seductive power, has recently devoted an illustrated booklet to her (in an appendix, in a first draft). Last season, at the great ball which takes place during Carnival, at the sports stadium, the immense velodrome still too small that day for the crowds who wanted to enter it, amongst the thousands and thousands she was the most noticed and even took the first prize, thanks to her 'Mother and daughter' costume, so naturally 'little old lady' on one side, 'little girl' on the other, so that she seemed to be made from two different pieces of time, joined by an invisible solder.

Frau Dr also has a whole collection of photographs and articles which she will take pleasure in showing to Vagualame, while Herr Dr continues to receive his clients. Vagualame, following her into the filing room, asks her if she knows Paris. Frau Dr exclaims: Paris, but she was born there, lived there for years, even got married there the first time and there gave birth to a charming daughter, Sea Lady, who will be happy to show the Berlin curiosities to a compatriot once she is out of Professor Cerf-Mayer's Institute, where she has just had a very strange operation.

Vagualame wonders what 'a very strange operation' can consist of for someone who wears so light-heartedly such a contradictory facial combination. But he doesn't have long to wonder, for there comes an avalanche of questions about Paris, its fashions, its theatres, to which Frau Dr doesn't even wait for the answers, she chatters as much as her twin, realises Vagualame, who, after all that Yolande has told him, has no trouble in discovering that the daughters of the coachman resemble each other as closely as do on the one hand an advertisement for a dye provided with a hairy scaffolding, white on the right, black on the left, and on the other hand, an ice statue.

An expressionist in Berlin as she was years ago, an Ibsen-follower in Paris, Frau Dr is one of those numerous women of good will who roam the world wearing medieval dresses, their hair in rolled-up pigtails over their ears, pearls of painted wood arranged into necklaces etc.… and, according to the current fashion, do pyrography, leather sculpting, spiritualism, or physical jerks, completely naked in the fields, where they are perfectly happy to be photographed leaping over hedges for the illustrated magazines of central Europe.

In the cities, in the studios where they comb anaemic angels against a background clutter of palm trees and lights, bind blue and pink English poets in Gothic style, in the same way as in the fields, when they gather the most innocent of flowers to make wreaths and garlands, everywhere and always, they claim devilishly to be vegetarians, mad about shows with art and rhythmic dances, speak ecstatically and enigmatically about Bach and Rimbaud, whom they call Johann Sebastian and Jean Arthur, as if they were just unimportant Jewish cousins who had managed to slide an unusual forename between their real banal one and the patronymic Levy. Chaste and peaceful creatures who would never refuse to take up arms to defend a liberty which no one is challenging.

Thus Frau Dr, a slave of her Privatdozent to the extent of serving as an advertisement with her before-and-after face, feels the need to loudly proclaim to Vagualame her principles concerning sexual rights. Previously a woman (Frau Dr indicates with her finger the wrinkled half of her symbolic forehead) was a domestic. Today, she is beginning to find her freedom (she strokes the other half, restored, young, smooth). There survive, from the barbaric times, just a few wives who still submit to the weekly conjugal coitus which makes them mothers without giving time for them to become lovers. But it is not over. Facts, you need facts and not simply theories, if you want customs to become what they should be. That's why Frau Dr is very happy that her daughter has had an operation at Dr Optimus Cerf-Mayer's sexual Institute that will change her most secret intimacy in whatever way she wishes.

As it happens Frau Dr has promised her daughter to go and see her this very afternoon.

So, if Vagualame has nothing better to do, let him come with her.

The Sexual Institute of Dr Optimus Cerf-Mayer.

A sort of ministry building with fake porphyry columns, staircases in pompous bad taste, opened packs of brochures lying on the floor, and in the niches, two artists' bronzes, one a naked moustachioed gentleman, the other a lady of the same height in the same attire.

Dr Optimus has just left in fact, but his dearest disciple will receive Vagualame and will show him the curiosities of the establishment, whilst Frau Dr will go to the post-operative floor to see her daughter.

The dearest disciple, a Swiss man (another one) speaks of Optimus Cerf-Mayer with tears in his voice. And certainly, how without someone with a master's degree in sexual matters, could the young man from the mountains find himself again, a young man who even before puberty had felt perverse instincts awakening in a flesh which one would have thought hereditarily tough and impermeable to vices? Abnormal. He was abnormal. And in canton Vaud they were speaking of sterilising those who were abnormal. He, with his tastes, certainly had no chance of making children. So he could oppose the uselessness of sterilisation. All the same, he shivered when the law about abnormality was discussed. A skylark amongst penguins (he had found that image himself), he would have liked to sing, to love. He did not dare, inhibited by the saintly

144

example of his family and especially of his elder sister, an elite creature, whose virtue had recently been feted (amazing, how this comes back) the length of *The Heart of the Goitrous Woman*.

As the last child of elderly parents, no doubt his blood was of a poorer quality, since he was the only one of the household to remain without goitre. His mother, who considered him to be rather frail, would certainly not have continued to surround him with gentle compassion if she had imagined what temptations kept him awake at night, with his heart beating in unison with the national cuckoo, in his little white bed. Perhaps he himself, through his struggles, might have finally smothered the voice of his senses, if fate had not one fine day decided to bring over a cousin from Zurich for his holidays.

The Zuricher, a great dandy, made quite an impression, thanks to his butter-coloured gloves, which he wore all the time except, precisely, for eating and sleeping. In love with the dandy and his gloves the young mountain boy took them all for a walk and when there were a few fir trees between them and the family home, he stroked the gloved hands of the city boy whose response was to crush the mountain boy's lips with his teeth. Stop. They lay down on the grass, but suddenly the Zuricher, who seemed to take pleasure in playing games, abandoned his partner in mid-stream and cried: "Blumen, Blumen." Flowers, flowers. It was the miracle of saffron, the very opposite of what Vagualame saw driving the mimosa sellers mad. Blumen. Blumen. Flowers, flowers whose innocence shames the flesh, all flesh. The Zuricher is to be a pastor, but before leaving for the theology school he offers his butter-coloured gloves, the profane gloves, the guilty gloves, to the mountain boy who has never had gloves for his reddened hands.

An equivocal gift which is enough to give rise to a stubborn fetishism.

The following winter there is an avalanche, whose torrent, along with the house, its bears carved out of wood, the statue of William Tell also of carved wood which protected the honest little people, carries away also the butter-coloured gloves.

We know that, thanks to the sacrifice of the elder sister, the chalet will be rebuilt.

But the gloves?

They are lost for ever.

From which arose the melancholy of Optimus's future disciple.

As the goitre of the Alpine Iphigenia had been paid for with its weight in gold, the adolescent will go to complete his studies in Neuchâtel.

Of course, he won't allow himself to be bewitched by the charm of the silent smokeless city. Yet at night his dreams take him to the lakeside.

The waters are green, but of a cold green pallor. A Balzac in length and breadth, he parades his belly, his frock coat with its crumpled tails, his trousers in need of pressing on the small hill where he is to meet Mme Hanska. Mme Hanska arrives. Very lovely. A small bonnet, a long flimsy veil, her feet wrapped in black fabric. A taffeta jacket the colour of dead leaves, a muslin skirt with flounces, small white and black flowers on a rust-coloured background. Unfortunately, there is the countess's blood flowing from the wide sleeves which although naturally blue nevertheless stains her exquisite travelling outfit. The lady bows to the cordial novelist. A wicked little gust of wind comes off the surface of the water, lifting the skirt's flounces, and Balzac has eyes only for the stockings of the same dark blue as the noble blood. Mme Hanska for the moment has many other worries. Rather intimidated (a psychologist will note how exquisite awkwardness can be in a person of such high standing) she apologises for no longer having any hands attached to her wrists. Just now, in the coach as she was trying to arrange her hair, with her hat and the tulle all floating around, she put so much energy into removing her gloves that the fingers and palms left along with the pretty butter-coloured chamois leather from which she was trying to free them.

Don't worry about that, says Balzac. I've got good enough big paws to fashion you a pair of handcuffs. And then you are, and always will be

Hanska, Hanska, the beautiful woman from Poland.

And, to a music box tune, Balzac now starts to dance, doing entrechats so clumsily that he turns into one of the wooden carved bears of the family chalet. The bear and chalet are carried away by a new avalanche and, with them, all the hands with their butter-coloured coquetries.

At this point of the dream the disciple of Dr Optimus wakes with a start.

Finally he confides in a young Romanian, as handsome as an antique cowherd, who has come to study child psychology which is brilliantly researched and taught at the university in Neuchâtel.

The Romanian advises a short stay at Optimus Cerf-Mayer's Institute. He himself, deep in Wallachia, was so miserable before he decided to go to consult the Berlin scientist for whom it was a game to see deep into this son of the Gospodars, since he proved to him then and there that all his hang-ups had their origin in his thus far unsatisfied desire to sleep with a woman who had a penis.

So the Swissy takes a ticket for Berlin.

Cerf-Mayer opens wide his arms and the doors of his palace to him. On the spot he sends for two pairs of butter-coloured gloves: one, which the young worrier will wear night and day, the other to be displayed in the Institute's museum of various fetishes, including the boots of a eonistic negro, that is to say similar to the Chevalier d'Éon,[1] known for never having worn the clothes of his sex. Like many male eonists this negro had a weakness for boots which he had made with very high

1 A celebrated 18th-century soldier, diplomat and spy, the Chevalier d'Éon lived openly as a man and as a woman.

heels in aviator style, which was in fashion during the war on both sides of the front, when the most delicate young girls copied the old soldiers, for eonism often gets complicated, the man dressing as a woman pushing perversity to the point of wanting to seem like a young woman falling for other women and, to seduce them more effectively, taking on a more or less masculine bearing.

The Swissy, according to Cerf-Mayer, was comparing himself to the Lady Hanska of his dream, and, if he had not stopped himself, would have been wearing a muslin skirt with flowery white and black flounces on a rust-coloured background, a taffeta jacket the colour of dead leaves, a bonnet and a long veil of the same disturbing green as the waters of the lake. It should be noted too that he was in love with Balzac, since he had invented the clumsy dance in order to confuse him with the bear, the first symbol of virility to move a budding homosexual in a chaste chalet.

But since his unacknowledged desire for a gentleman with a large belly has brought him here Dr Optimus, very generously, offers his own chubby person.

Having become 'the dearest disciple', our Swissy will forget the peaks and forests in order to devote himself body and soul to the works of his master.

So he hurries to give Vagualame the house questionnaire, two pages whose delicate and insidious print enquires about tastes, capacities, dimensions, anomalies and petty details of the distinctive signs. That done, he speaks about article 175 of the German penal code which punishes with prison a man who has relations with a young boy. To tell the truth article 175 does not make much difference. Cerf-Mayer, who has never lacked courage, has nevertheless for a long time carried out such a strenuous campaign for its abolition that the Bavarian nationalists, in Munich, in 1919 made an attempt on his life.

And if, the Swissy adds, the majority of people care very little about article 175, some unlucky people, lovers of the open air, surprised several times at night by the police in the Tiergarten and because of their recidivism condemned to a fairly long incarceration, on leaving their prison cell come more often than you would believe to ask Cerf-Mayer for a formally drawn up certificate to permit their castration. A very simple operation. Less serious than a common appendicitis.

Vagualame would prefer to think about something else, but the Swissy, happy to feel sheltered from a legal sterilisation with which canton Vaud threatens its inhabitants, grumbles about the advantages acquired willingly by eunuchs. Men, it appears, are not the only ones to benefit from the help of the cutting iron, and women too have a great taste for the ablations which make changes to their private parts.

"Thus, the daughter of Frau Dr Herzog, Sea Lady, submissive to the wishes of a beautiful American woman, Miss Patre, her lover, was not afraid to have her bosom filed down and to have removed what the young misogynist Helvetian calls, as if it were a question of a hopping family of very young and sweet animals: the ovaries. A young man, finding that a part of what the young girl had been relieved of would suit him very well, came to the Institute so that he could have a graft of…"

"The breasts?" interrupts the simplistic Vagualame.

"No, the ovaries" the Swissy corrects him, "and in fact they have grafted them onto his right hip."

"A pretty sight."

No doubt Frau Dr Herzog is right, and everyone has the right to do with themself, their body, their face as they wish, but why did an American woman, accustomed by the transatlantic fashion for camping to sleeping on the hard ground, have to persuade the Redhead to turn herself into a board, the Redhead whom Vagualame at Mme Rosalba's instigation has come to ask to let herself become pregnant with a blue child?

He weeps for the ovaries, as the Swissy says, the ovaries snatched from their nests for an exile on the right hip of a ladies' man, crazy babies, tiddly babies, my little shellfish keen on absinthe, clams of love, kingfishers, starlings, ovaries, more touching than your patronymic cousins the young otaries, the Otariidae, dear girls snatched from the original delicious ice fields to play the violin or the hunting horn in the dust of music halls, between a Japanese tightrope walker's number and the efforts of a couple of syphilitic acrobats in purple leotards with faded underarms.

But the family of the ovaries of a Sea Lady are elsewhere than on the ice floes and, in the Mediterranean for example, the whole troop would be affianced to a community of sea urchins.

At table, during dessert on the day of the communal wedding, they'll have sung:

Ursula, Ursuline
Mr Urchin
Ursa the bear, your cousin
Has his marine son
Long live the mariners
And glory to the sea urchin

In Polynesia, half-algae, half coral, they would have blossomed, a mineral vegetation and worthy of those trees of salt you find deep down below the earth hidden away in mines. Now, as plants, even plants, these ovaries would not have wanted your pollen, Vagualame, great orchid that you are. The blue child? But he was a chimera, amongst the chimeras of the delirious fortune-teller of the lower middle-classes. As the father of an azure baby you would not have been unhappy. Blessed genetic instinct. You are ashamed. You feel frustrated, diminished. A strange morality, the polished story of the Redhead. The Swissy speaks. You listen without hearing. You stick to your plan, grotesquely. Growing testy. Plays on words now. But, on a beach of skin, to right of a belly button, the ovaries have deserted Sea Lady.

Now, out of all that, what could the great Scandinavian have thought, he under whose protection had been placed through her forename the young woman who had been operated on? What would the distinguished old man with the misty beard say, this creator who was able to conjure up from the fog a whole people of photographers drunk on hyposulfite, architects whose houses refused to stay upright, those at the point of death, those with ataxia, shady financiers, unacceptable pregnant women, young mothers of families losing their heads simply by dancing a tarantella at Mardi Gras, I ask you again, what would he say, he who in the houses of the festive town as well as in the deserted countryside or a lonely fjord knew how to remove you from these cases of conscience with a more or less alpine pride, what would he reply if he heard the Swissy announcing that Sea Lady would soon be painted naked, with her bosom as the operation has simplified it, that is to say, without the slightest shadow of breasts, right in the middle of the wall of the Sexual Institute?

Well, Papa Ibsen, if these emaciated gentlemen, these delicate flowers of hysteria,
their companions and the syphilitic adolescents for whom you have the same weakness
as the Swiss woman for her goitrous men,
if your Heddas, Eilerts, Oswalds and company and you yourself had heard the story
of the high-heeled boots and the one about
the butter-coloured gloves, would you not
at that point have found that the epilepsy of
the frockcoated gentlemen, the megalomania
of a contractor of public works, the delirious
words of a virgin in the process of spoiling
a stage floor with the blows of an alpenstock
to the rhythm of her speech, the ravings of a
very well brought-up lady at the water's edge,
are nothing, after all, but chicken feed, for it's
another song when, at the end of the world,
the flesh howls for real.

Optimus Cerf-Mayer, it's easy to make fun
of him.

But who better to help the creatures lost in
the forest of cries and the stakes likely to tear
their dermis and epidermis, and the whole epithelium, internal and external, and the bone
marrow, the precious bone marrow? Common
people, when they say of someone who masturbates that he'll blow his brains out, as if

every skull should empty out in a great river of lukewarm opaline. And what waves upon this river, flowing thickly nevertheless. The wind that raises them is called neither foehn, nor mistral, nor sirocco. It overturned the heaviest rafts of desire. Desperate chords, heartrending arpeggios, so that you'd believe that all the nerves were being torn out of living bodies. I can hear yelping, weeping, raging, insulting loudly, with the loudest voice on earth, a voice, Papa Ibsen who will not allow himself to season it with symbolic sauce.

Have you now understood the title of this book, and why you're being asked:

Are you all crazy?

An example to take from the mass of Cerf-Mayer's documents, the photograph of a young man who gives the impression of being correct and prudent (it's about the Prince of Wales again) who is not afraid to dress as a woman and to have his photograph taken like that, and to remember that this portrait of a petticoated man appeared quite innocently on the front page of a perfectly respectable Parisian magazine[1], is that not enough to make one give up on studying men, at least according to the classical method, which boasted of getting to the very heart of the mystery by means of experience and reasoning?

Lady Psychology, that stuck-up woman, let us call her Emma once and for all, and not speak of her again. You, Papa Ibsen, we need to give you credit for finding her ugly enough to want her veiled. So the silly girl with blue stockings arriving in the country of fjords boarded one of those small steamships that take the post. You, captain of a mediocre ship, you watched the night falling whilst your passenger was arranging her tulles and gauzes with the same gestures as the Hanska woman at the edge of the Neuchâtel Lake. Captain Ibsen, Cap' Ibs', as the ship's boy says, you begin to reflect. Now this apparition gesticulating (Goodness! What vitality!) over there, in the family home, don't you think, Capt' Ibs', that he would do better to properly kiss, there where one can hear her desire, the young servant girl at whose birth her late father did not find himself a complete stranger? But the

---

1 Excelsior (author's note).

old mother, a brave Scandinavian whose ideas have little to fear from currents of air beneath the eiderdown of white hair which protects them, have with the relentlessness of unhappy virtues for years and years waited in silence for the moment when they could speak of all they had in their hearts, she speaks, she speaks. And she rattles on and on. Her son tries to quieten her, but, poor young man, his strength abandons him. He doesn't even want to sleep with the maid any longer. He wants the sun. He's offered a glass of water. He dies. That's life. The apparition will not reappear.

From the depths of her grief the lady with the respectable hair style is already regretting not having left things to work themselves out which would certainly not have failed to be surprising, if she had permitted her dear departed one make a extra-fraternal acquaint-ance with the illegitimate servant. He could have allowed himself to follow illustrious predecessors, Byron for example, who was, as everyone knows, his sister's lover, an influence which would, besides, have risked dragging away the cerebral and nervous young man since flesh unsatisfied by incest, the insatiable clubfoot (these cripples, all the same, what temperaments!) gave himself up to a series of new accursed love affairs, with, amongst others, a young Italian doctor, with profile like that on a medal, hair long enough to wrap round his head with also a small bun at the back, and whose sculpted bust with its natural grandeur has a place of honour in the Museum of the Sexual Institute, between the empty panel, intended for Sea Lady, and the one covered by a painting in official colours showing the attempt on the life of Cerf-Mayer.

In this museum are shown all sorts of sadisms, masochisms, fetishisms, onanisms, the infinite variety of ruts and couplings, either schematised by some graphic scientist or fixed as precisely as possible in one of the aspects of their changing movements in photographs, pictures, drawings.

A magnificent choice of whips, chains, torture beds should be noted too, for those fond of English education, a nice variety of sex dolls, large and small phalluses and Chinese instruments for revitalising failing virilities, all of it as well labelled and ordered as a collection of butterflies or minerals.

Looking at so many photographs, where creatures are no more than cogs in the machinery of sensuality, whether it's a question of men and men, of women and women, of men and women, of shepherds and goats, of girls and wolf dogs, Vagualame can see how Leda and her swan were able, as a scandalous couple, to become subjects for alabaster statuettes, for honourable bronze clocks.

To gather together such a quantity of documents, Cerf-Mayer must have sent around the world a whole army of secret agents who were scattered round brothels, houses of ill repute, bourgeois toilets, steam baths, holds of war ships and merchant ships, public gardens at shady times, lobbies of music halls and cinemas where temptations rub up against temptations, barracks' sleeping quarters, the reserved areas, quays, docks of ports, the backs of provincial shops, schools' dormitories, and above all the streets, the streets which never end and which are taken, not in the figurative sense, the streets taken as their groups of roaming whores would wish to do when the pavements, the roadway, thought to be empty a minute ago by the man in a hurry to get home, have suddenly with a darkness deeper than the night, with a strange dance down on the tarmac, reawakened the desires of, forced to stiffen, to live, the flesh which wanted nothing more than sleep, oblivion, death.

Thanks to the devotion of his collaborators, Cerf-Mayer has been able to draw up lists, statistics, establish for example the approximate number of men who don't need another mouth than their own to satisfy what, in themselves, takes pleasure particularly in being tickled by the tip of a bold tongue.

And certainly, Dr Optimus's police haven't done badly, since in the dossier of the English heir to the throne the Swissy has found a photograph of the bedspread embroidered for Yolande.

Vagualame plays at being curious, as if he knows nothing.

Questioned about Yolande, the Swissy after examining the archives replies that she is a big fraud. He speaks of the fakir, whose exact use he doesn't suspect, nor that of the rat, of the bull.

Two days after his visit to the Sexual Institute, Vagualame receives a card from Cerf-Mayer inviting him to an eonism séance in honour of Sea Lady, back on her feet and now with permission to dress as a man.

The eonism séance.

Frau Dr Herzog in the first row.

Vagualame next to her.

A very serious audience who applaud Cerf-Mayer to the rafters when he appears.

The master greets them and begins a chat which repeats more or less all that the Swissy has already said.

Then comes the procession of the mannequins.

First, the birth of eonism, incomplete, as represented by a young man wearing normal clothes but with a blue satin beret on his head, with a small pink feather, like a kiss curl on his plaster-like cheek. The next one wears short trousers with petticoats, thanks to which his skinny leg appears even more pitiful, encased in a black silk stocking. The third has a stole of peeled rabbit skin draped over a skimpy sleeve. As for the fourth, a strangler's hands, a butcher's neck, he drops his jacket and trousers, and emerges all floating and flimsy, silks and laces, a crêpe de chine blouse, a bra of tulle with incredible mauve ribbons on the torso of a wrestler.

And now the little pièce de resistance: a large timid lady who comes forward and in her softest voice confesses that she was once an uhlan[1]. He'd always enjoyed dressing as a woman, and after the war had had himself castrated in order to fit better into his dresses. After the last hair of his beard had fallen from his chin, with his body fattened and rounded, she is really happy. During the week she works in a factory producing chemicals. On Sundays, to amuse herself, she does small needlework jobs. She takes from her bag place mats, table napkins, doilies. Very gallantly, Cerf-Mayer offers her his arm to go to from the platform into the hall, where the spectators are enjoying buying the embroideries.

At last, here comes Sea Lady.

Beautiful, despite the brush which makes up her hair and her clothes like those of a check-in clerk.

Neither man nor woman, as her mother is neither young nor old, or Yolande, neither dead nor alive, the last of a line which, in a single person, was able on several occasions to bring together irreducible opposites, she thanks the director and the surgeon of the Sexual Institute in the name of those men who should have been born women and those women who should have been born men.

---

1 Uhlans were initially Lithuanian, later also Polish, light cavalry units primarily armed with a lance.

Vagualame is the only one not to applaud.

Another word from Frau Dr Herzog, a mother without prejudice, who permitted the delicate operation, and the whole room falls about.

Sea Lady, acknowledging the applause, then sits beside Optimus.

Miss Patre enters.

The beautiful American, looking like one from a Douglas Fairbanks film, and having escaped from Hollywood's most medieval cavalcade, before singing her Scottish ballads also makes her little speech.

She considers it her duty that no one who takes an interest in sexuality should be unaware of how after obtaining from her puritan family the right to leave Massachusetts for Europe, this amazon of the Boston suburbs came to Berlin where, wishing to study libido, she managed to find the most wonderful opportunity in the world. Descended from the Patres (there are none more Mayflower), the young woman had seen her luck change at home. First her old father. No doubt he continued to sign bank notes, but one very cold day the wind froze his right eye, which since then has been harder than ice and dry, unseeing. "Well," said the old father, when he came back home blind in one eye. "Well," repeated the old father, without even taking advantage of the continuing susceptibility to the damp of the ruined look in order to shed a few tears. "Well," and he poured himself a double serving of whisky. They think he's become an alcoholic. The mother. An intellectual. She was the one who insisted on giving her daughter the forename Cleo in memory of an empress whose patronym Patre makes a final echo. Mrs Patre never loses her 'nobility', even when with her limbs looser than those of a frog, she swims in the clear streams. Mad about 'modernity', as soon as *Within a Budding Grove*[1] was published she organised a whole series of lectures about Marcel Proust and the idea of friendship, which Dick, the elder brother of Cleo, made great fun of. Dick was a wicked boy anyway, who had previously tried to rape his sister. Cleo did not let it happen, for she was in love with her female cousin in New York, Maggy, the best-dressed woman in the world who goes to Paris every two months to buy dresses at Poiret's and, at Cartier's, bracelets that she smuggles past the customs

1 The second volume of Proust's *A la Recherche du Temps Perdu—A l'ombre des jeunes filles en fleurs*. (The title shown here is from the translation of the work by C K Moncrieff.)

checks in tubes of toothpaste. Ashamed of her passion for the best-dressed woman in the world, Cleo confides in Mammy, who does not really seem to understand and replies that the Virgin Mary and the mother of Saint John the Baptist, also two cousins, were so fond of each other that too many scruples would insult their memory. The old father with one eye when consulted said "Well." Then Cleo goes to see Dick. Dick doesn't understand anything other than incest, in which he considers himself an expert since he has perverted the younger son, judiciously baptised Junior. But the family ties between Cleo and Maggy are too loose for Dick to be able to give any advice at all, and Cleo goes off to find the great Cerf-Mayer, dear Optimus, who has so greatly helped her flight towards liberty that now she is ready to leap across the ocean of prejudice in a single bound, a single one.

A small comparison with the aerial crossing of the Atlantic and the salute to Europe in response to the greeting which the gentleman La Fayette went off in former times to take to the future United States of America.

Not worrying about a political digression Miss Patre conjures up the great shade of Woodrow Wilson, sponsoring this celebration (a date in the history of the confraternity of nations) since three of them are collaborating here: France, which in the person of Sea Lady inspired by Miss Patre, that is to say by America, has willingly submitted her body to the scientific effrontery of young Germany represented by Cerf-Mayer and his collaborators.

For the journalists taking notes in the hall, Miss Patre announces that she'll be staying in Berlin for a few more months, before returning to America accompanied by Sea Lady who, when there, like Frau Dr Herzog here who with her before-and-after face has served as a living advertisement for her husband, will be the proof to be used for the massive publicity which it is well time to put into place around *sexual liberation*.

Now, since everything this evening has to be fun, happy, and since Miss Patre is dressed as a young Robin Hood, she's going to sing a song for which the unfortunate Mary Stuart, Queen of Scots, composed both words and music for one of her servant woman of whom she was very fond. The Swissy will accompany her. The cross-dressing former uhlan, the large lady in green who played the fife whilst she was a soldier, will turn the pages.

Arpeggios, soft cooings, and voice exercises.

The celebration in honour of Sea Lady ends in the most musical euphoria.

Whilst Miss Patre is away changing her medieval togs for the international uniform of modern Sapphos, Frau Dr Herzog introduces her daughter to Vagualame and invites him to spend the rest of the evening with them. The Swissy, who boasts of knowing a "schön lokal", is assigned as his accompanying servant by Dr Optimus, who has to work all night on a study of the perversions and erotic abuses of the Patagonians, according to notes made by explorers.

They're about to set off for the Swissy's schön lokal and the door is already open when out of a taxi jumps a tall, pale young woman dressed in black. With great expressions of friendship she throws herself upon Frau Dr Herzog and Sea Lady. Vagualame recognises Yolande, who apologises for not arriving in time for the eonism séance. She has just arrived by train. There is just enough time to install her in the hotel along with her companions, the fakir, the rat and the apartment bull, her beloved trio which tomorrow she will introduce to the Wintergarten.

Frau Dr Herzog questions her about the dresses she has brought from Paris, but Yolande only wants to talk about a diamond-studded bolero and a very voluminous tulle skirt which ends at the knees in front, and trails several metres at the back, scintillating all over with black sequins, tiny stars in response to the electric ones clustering over the Wintergarten ceiling. Imagining her thus dripping beneath blurry billows, her upper body squeezed into shining armour, Cerf-Mayer wonders what the vice of this nocturnal ballerina could be. There is certainly a mystery between her on the one hand and on the other the man and the animals of ridiculous proportions around her.

As the Director of the sexual Institute of a capital city, where the cold winter sun brings into blossom the slender Jewish women and the blond athletes, as the spring sunshine does with the Montmorency cherry trees, Dr Optimus knows that the wings of music hall stages are deeper and contain more dubious cargos than do the holds of great ships.

A bee, a drop of gold, sensuality needs other calyxes than the ostrich feather suns, no longer very fresh, or the corollas of tarlatan obligingly transparent to gentle nudity. The bee, a drop of gold, buzzing, not bloated but delicately intoxicated on an invisible sap, gets excited, knocks against the black velvet walls, against the background of which, whiter than the earthenware pipes of the travelling stalls, blossoms the cold geometry of the trapeze artists, the embarrassing seductiveness of the conjurors, the pale blue charm of the medium-like and definitely diabolical women, the jokes of the jugglers and the enigmatic brass of the animal-tamers and the lions.

Cerf-Mayer is not unaware of the fact that the Hercules with the smiles of young girls, with their most correct white gardenias on the lapels of their tailcoats, who play ball with the seals must have started by gradually seducing the whole colony, for these oily clowns only obey pretty boys when their slow flesh has been aroused, penetrated with caresses which are simultaneously the sharpest and the strongest.

So, Yolande with the fakir, the rat and the bull…

It's a shame that Cerf-Mayer has this work which can't wait any longer. He would have followed the little group which Miss Patre has at last just dragged away, Miss Patre who has reappeared without the hose and doublet which she has exchanged for a skirt and a jacket tailored like a man's.

So the dearest disciple has promised to watch with all eyes, to listen with all ears.

✳

The 'schön lokal' of the Swissy.

First he shows Vagualame the washbasins where a carefully handwritten notice forbids the sale of cocaine, kisses on the mouth between persons of the same sex, furtive fumbling, caresses with the fingers, exercises with lips, all the things in fact which an inno-cent-looking cigarette seller has just suggested.

But a drum roll and the Swissy urges Vagualame to go to rejoin their companions, for it's Micky's dance, and Micky...

In the hall.

A miserable dance hall, cheerless.

Another drum roll.

The Swissy claps his hands, licks his chops: "Micky, here's Micky."

The cross-dressing former uhlan, the large maker of chemical products, would look like a sylph compared with Micky, an adipose sexagenarian, an obese little bourgeois, ruined by the taxi drivers who beat him, resolutely greenish beneath the blood red of his lips, the coal covering his eyelids, eye lashes and eyebrows, the crushed brick make-up of his cheeks, and the lumpy starch plastering his forehead, chin, and neck, his arms sticking out of the sleeveless dress with its square décolletage, a copy of the one which the Empress Josephine wore on her coronation day. To finish off the Empire-style ensemble, a wig with silver paper diadems, twisted around the curls, ringlets and kiss-curls, the drop earrings, the necklaces and chains made from the stoppers of bottles of mineral water, espadrilles serving as buskins, seams of cotton wool stained with ink to look like ermine along a rag of red panne velvet showing off the scarlet of a cloak worn by the young men of the court.

Micky and his following cross the room.

The orchestra accompanies the greetings of the imperial caricature. She stops, the old curtain serving as a train is removed. In its place are brought castanets, a bunch of carnations, some black lace that she arranges as a mantilla, a shawl of many colours, a fan. Now a young Spanish woman, one hand holding up her petticoat, Micky is ready for the most devilish saraband. All that's missing (and that's a case of force majeure, since they would collapse beneath her weight) are the high heels. The orchestra plays music by Granados. The incomparable Andalusian hums to herself "Tanz pompeux, tanz gracieux". Trying to whirl her hundred kilos around she loses her balance, finds it again, loses it again, and boom, boom, boom, "tanz gracieux, tanz pompeux", she invents chimeric ways to seduce an imaginary toreador.

Once the number is finished Yolande issues an invitation to the imperialistic Andalusian, who declines: 'She' is a little nervous…

"What a nuisance," complains Yolande. "I would have liked to introduce my apartment bull to this Carmen."

Obedient to Optimus's instructions, the Swissy begs:

"Madame, madame, I would so much love to meet the bull."

Yolande looks the Swissy up and down.

"It's not the bull's time, young man, not the time to disturb him, and for you it will never be the time to speak about him. And now is not the time for anything, for anybody."

"I thought for you it was always the bull's time. When you cherish…"

"Did I ask you if you enjoy rubbing up against heifers, you little calf? Instead of your indiscretions, model yourself on M Vagualame's reserve."

On the dance floor, open again to the public, Miss Patre and Sea Lady are twirling, entwined together.

"They're so lovely," sighs Frau Dr Herzog.

"Exquisite, adorable," Yolande goes further (and in an aside to Vagualame): "Have you lost your tongue? Why this silence?"

"Were you not praising my reserve a moment ago?"

"A way of speaking. I pity you. Poor little chap. You've allowed yourself to be so influenced by Rosalba. To have come all this way to see her whom you wished to impregnate with a blue child dancing in the arms of a ridiculous American woman! My perfect vengeance, Vagualame."

The orchestra stops.

The dancers have gone back to their seats.

Nobody is saying anything.

The Swissy, not wanting to go home empty-handed, asks the assembled company:

"Are you sadists or masochists?"

"Both sadist and masochist at the same time," replies Yolande in the name of the universe, for no-one remembers if he started out by torturing in hope of brutalities which, as a fair response, would scar him body and soul, or whether, on the contrary, spontaneously, he offered this body and this soul, naked, without any protective undergarments, because he needed a pretext for inflicting his vengeance of flowery bruises spangled with stars of blood.

Sea Lady and Miss Patre (was it the passionate tones of the woman with the fakir that aroused their appetite?) speak of their tiredness and leave, entrusting the whole group to a friend they have just introduced to them, a young woman from Berlin who has been seen at the earliest of dawns out walking, never tired, exploring the capital whose immense night she loves, this busy night, more electric in its haste than those shining posters which decorate it, embellished by young women who are not weighed down by the furs they wear and the crystals streaming from the sky in great clear waves, from the cinema entrances, from the streetlamps, from the houses which are never tired, in order to wash—but who then has pressed the enormous and invisible sponges?—to wash the tiredness from this giant city with its stonework skin and its adolescent breath.

This skin, this breath, no ordeals change them, even over in the north, where sadness, hunger, anguish beat their carpets all blessed day long.

Yet this misery, this toughness, strikes heads with great blows of a hammer, it hollows out its galleries, and like scabies, like a virus, like a devil woman with a poisoned fingernail, scratches the fragile skin of earth beneath the greenish stubble of the squares, grinds its pepper, pours its vitriol between the thighs of the suburbs. Then, deep in the night clubs, the young ones with their hands in their pockets are scratching away, drawing blood. There is not only the international prostitution of fake sailors, fake young boys in cyclists' jerseys, but also the obligatory one of the kids who don't want to starve to death and are shivering, outside, for real, with no shirts between their old jackets of poor cloth and their shoulders, backs and chests.

In the bars where they go, as night falls, their heads hurt because of the heat and the desires which they constantly have to try to feign. There is dust everywhere. Now, the suffocating greyness, the muddy mica up against the pink power of the ingénue, only the young girl can pierce their transparency like that of a dirty curtain, as the circus horsewoman pierces the hoop of white paper placed as an obstacle in her path.

She enters, her cheeks and hands frozen from the night air, and the boys, squeezing her fingers in their large paws, are already feeling they are no longer in danger of passing away, of becoming as shiftily colourless as the room whose atmosphere, its *Stimmung*, is moreover exciting the clients much more, much better than all the young ones amongst whom they trawl without even looking at them.

The friend of Sea Lady and Miss Patre, having listed the various attractions and specialities of these places, has on the contrary opted for what the Swissy calls a 'lesbique lokal'.

The lesbique lokal has nothing seductive about it, any more than have its tubby dimpled owners, Frida and Mina, 'very like best men' with carnations in the buttonholes of their trimmed jackets, their large breasts sacrificed beneath their cuirasses of starched underwear.

Frida and Mina approach, asking for news of Sea Lady. Frau Dr Herzog requests them to sit down, and in the proud tones of a mother boasting of her daughter's qualities, her domestic talents and her promising piano playing, describes the eonism séance.

For her part, Yolande invents some preposterous lies for the Swissy, who drinks in her every word.

The young lady from Berlin dances.

Then Vagualame, to himself:

Now is the moment for soliloquies. Alone and like an old rag you float on a great tide of sadness. Instead of turning round to confront the waves galloping behind you and already biting your heels, you continued on your way, entertained by objects, by marionettes, attracted by any old drop of water which the first ray of sun to arrive transformed for the joy of your frivolity into an illusory prism, a meaningless kaleidoscope. And remember, you cheat, when you were unhappy, feeling let down or spitting blood, you invented for yourself some hypocritical consolations, the most common of which consisted of telling yourself that the picture was inside yourself. But scarcely were you out of your misery than you went off in search of some new labyrinth of funny things.

The whole clique—the Rosalbas around the world who, to exact vengeance on their sooty Les Batignolles, called themselves fortune tellers and flung their pots of threats; all the women with fakirs; the Patatas in love with their toy twins and ready to give them up for thirty pairs of male Indians; the beautiful goitrous women and their Swissy brothers; Frau Dr Herzog with her before-and-after face; Balzac and Madame Hanska, Ibsen and Emma Psychology, and another Emma, Emma Bovary, Flaubert's one (another eonist, and who claimed *I am Madame Bovary*); the Sea Ladies, well planed down,

> *Without buttocks or breasts.*
> *Like a Janeton doll,*

the Misses Patre called Cleo ; this whole clique—when you've carefully watched all their grimaces you wonder:

"What next?…"

"Next? Nothing."

The great tide of sadness draws back. It's left you at a dead end.

But this time, instead of going to question a fortune-teller in her cabinet, go rather and to put a few questions to the young German woman, your guide who has just come to sit by you. Ask her something or other. For example, what her name is.

Reply: She's nicknamed Carlina, because she looks like the dogs that were fashionable in the days of Louis XIV, such as you see on all the seventeenth century engravings.

You, Vagualame, you look like a Pekinese.

But don't go making a comparison just because of that.

Your chaos is not strength, whilst the young girl, despite some irregular features, doesn't deserve the very French insult of minois chiffonné[1].

So, you can't play at being a narcissist.

It's a shame, because confusing yourself with a potential object of your love, and then with this potential love, and then little by little with love itself, gives you an excellent opinion of yourself, and, after the Cerf-Mayer show with all those unhappy men and women desperate to get out of their own skin, you

----

1 A face which is pretty despite some imperfections— 'crumpled but cute' perhaps.

would very much like to feel at ease in your own. You detest your inner self, you reject it. But, the present?

The eyes of the young woman from Berlin, those eyes whose precise colour you have not even bothered to ascertain, you have succumbed to their charm. At the end of the evening, of your indecision, their redeeming light has appeared. Lightning falling from on high but which gently slips along your watery distress. And above all this electricity continues without stopping. Further than her, further than you, beyond her, beyond you there are you and she, there are you two.

You and she = you two.

Two syllables drawn together in a disturbing synthesis, but chemistry has many other mysteries. And then, the formulae, you have pockets full of them, your head full of them, your heart full of them. You feel well the earth of France, as the chauvinistic Rosalba used to say. Work on this proposition from the former flea trainer, think deeply and confess that you had a great talent for rhetoric. Your carelessness, your disarray were still practical, organised. If you wandered around the countryside it wasn't through lack of intelligence, but because no fatal law was in charge of your life.

So, why here rather than there, rather than elsewhere?

You do anything with anyone, anywhere, anyhow and you expect it to be a job well done.

Imagine a plain, a steppe, and on this plain, this steppe, a wind which is not from the north, nor the south, nor the east nor the west, but at the same time from the north and the south, from the east and the west, and also from the south-east and the north-west, from the north-east and the south-west.

The most fragile umbelliferous plants, those you puffed at when you were a child, are made martyrs by the whirlwind of contradictory forces which rolls them along but doesn't toss them into the air, for it can't send for more than a metre what your childish breath propelled up to the heavens.

So you, who tried without taking delight in them to love all the violence of the flesh and the spirit, thirsting for a witch's filter, keen on magic plants, words of incantatory charms, always ready to climb the five floors to the fortune-tellers of the suburbs who open wide the doors of the future onto tattered scarlet far-distant fairy-tale worlds, as in a springtime dawn with the windows of their hovels opening onto a sky, revived despite the thick smoke, you who wished for the most unbending cord and iron for the bow of your desires, which you hoped would send you, the arrow, up to the stars, you again, in the same place in the quiver, wriggling about like a grandiloquent epileptic, you find yourself more dressed up than those pompous raga-muffins, with feathered hats, frills and furbe-lows, flounces the colour of pigeons' throats, and lace of all ages and colours, like packets of old rags sleeping on the banks.

You dream of an earthquake, but like an anaemic dilettante you would have suffered from it like that old umbrella of Barrès did from a little shake.

And tell me, what is the point of the protocol of sensuality, knowing bodies, love in its thirty-two positions in all its forms and perversities; what is the point, again, of alcohol and drugs, which you've tried in many varieties if, when you've tried them, you hav-en't even developed what stage left calls vice and stage right calls passion? You are no less proud of an experience which would allow you to go for small carnal descriptions, very Baedecker-like, with a toe-curling naturalism. There are also the very slightly pharmaceutical considerations regarding artificial paradises, and I can hear chattering for hours and hours, conjuring up the great wild beasts which did not deign to make a prey of your defective and jumpy self. You gave up on your sickness when you saw, saw with your own eyes, how, on the highest floor of the skyscraper sanatorium, the silence, the immobility like shifty accomplices helped people to die. So for once you had the strength of your anger, too much strength for you to be content with a revolt on the spot, with a Kurhaus dance floor, where a young woman gave you the gift of a smile, a young woman more or less transparent, so slim, so tired, that she could no longer dance except with her feet on those of her dance partner, certainly less heavy than a falcon of medieval tales on the wrist of the hunter.

But, just because you refused your end high up in the cold, that doesn't mean you necessarily have more reasons to keep going.

You are in Berlin.

Why?

Answer, if you can.

You have nothing to say?

So, take off your mask.

Goodness, you look like a brother to me.

And, if you please, what was your name before the rue des Paupières-Rouges?

What did you say?… René Crevel?

But you are me. I am you. We are the same person.

So speaking of Vagualame, that is to say of René Crevel, I will not use the third person, any more than I will speak to him in the second.

But first, we must put an end to our other heroes, give them their fate.

Yolande, for example, leaving Frida and Mina's place, returned to her hotel which she had unwisely chosen in the neighbourhood of the Zoo, from where there were emanations, imperceptible to human nostrils, but which intoxicated her beloved animals. The rat weighing fifty kilos started nibbling the feet of the impassive fakir, whilst the apartment bull tried to disembowel him. But the wrinkled old man had led such a hard and ascetic life that the former broke his teeth and the latter his horns. Nevertheless, both stuck at it until not a crumb was left and Yolande found them well fed and fast asleep. She understood her misfortune, went to bed, and stoically, as if nothing was untoward, died at daybreak, and this time for good. There was a scandal, an investigation. There was talk of spying, or a matter of morals. Dr Optimus, appointed as an expert, was not able to come to a conclusion, and as neither the assassins nor the victim's actual civil status could be discovered, nor for good reason the fakir's place of refuge, suspicious from the first minute, the nationalist French press seized on the affair in order, of course, to talk about espionage. From which came a batch of fancy articles, concluding: Don't let us evacuate the Ruhr, let us wage war on Morocco. Let us mistrust fakirs, India, Asia, the whole of that Orient which claims to be impassive and mystical but which plays at Teutonic and Bolshevist imperialism. *Et tutti quanti*…

The apartment bull and the rat weighing fifty kilos, although in very poor condition, were taken in by the Zoo, but did not take long to die of consumption, because having become deeply masochistic they could not live, one without the spike of the horned hat, the other without the caresses of the mask with its metal jaws.

The Swissy continues to do the honours at the sexual Institute when his master is out walking.

In a week's time Frau Dr Herzog will accompany Sea Lady and Miss Patre to Hamburg. The two young women will set off for America where they are greatly needed to organise *sexual liberation*.

Mimi Patata has just discovered she is pregnant. She's no longer very young, no spring chicken, but nevertheless expects to give birth to at least a pair of twins.

I, Vagualame, René Crevel, I've come back to Paris.

They have built new houses in the rue des Paupières-Rouges. As a consolation I go round the fortune-tellers. I'm pressed to become serious and, instead of asking others, and myself: "Are you all crazy?", to finish a book about Diderot which I began work on years ago, or to start one about Berlin where, I readily state, all is perfect.

Well, the encyclopaedist can wait. As for the City, the beautiful Prussian, it doesn't need me. And then I wouldn't have the presumption to claim to know it after three months. Besides, it isn't there yet but is up and coming. A world where I finally met some youngsters, and especially one, all really pure whatever the fashionable activities, a purity which is not the word I'm trying here to make into a new snobbery, which people have tried to bring back into fashion by seasoning it with the sauce of scandal. But purity remains as much a stranger to scandal as is fatalism, scorning worldly and domestic considerations. Both one and the other, they despise plays on words, games of sex, of spirit, which are at the very least just fun and games until something goes wrong.

And then, what is the point of the amusements which gnaw away at our minutes, these nibblers (like the late Yolande's rat), but can't do anything about the hours, whose claws have scratched our sulphurous desert? There, they say, are oases that offer a gentle shade, palms, water fountains. But the sirocco sets alight the sky blue and pink of the friendliest lies. The water diviners, crouching beneath the gusts of fiery wind, travel the world which they fill with their cries of despair, for the hazel tree no longer obeys the water's voice. Besides, you men, there is no longer enough water for your thirst. The pavements with their heavy cobblestones with which you wanted to cover the very earth are cracking, bursting open, spreading dust like volcanoes suddenly erupting. Howls of terror! The first genuine happening for centuries and centuries. It's time to start again from the beginning, with the harsh ancestral anguish, and only the miracle of frankness can resurrect violence.

Violence. The very expression of that *need for supreme justice* of which André Breton speaks in his *Surrealist Manifesto* and without which something deep inside us, which cannot be mistaken, maintains that there could not exist a moral or intellectual life.

And for you all, in the sarcophaguses of your sophisticated relativism, in order to liberate your stiff bindings of quibbles and high-flown ideas, dynamite was needed, and dynamite, more dynamite to loosen your lips so greedily closed.

Condemned, executed, finished—the rhetoric, grimacing in prose and in verse, the shapes in the void and that formal harmony, meaninglessly, since it has not yet found its echo in the heart's silence. But already mouths are trembling, and their passionate stuttering proves that the truth is no more in wine than in the happy medium. So you, oh Mediterranean, the sea in the middle, your vines, your flowers, your perfumed kindnesses, the cosmetic colour of your red rocks, of your sun, your sensual deceptive edges, of a metal whose too clever carvings serve as coastlines to mirror the selfishness of civilisations, how can one be taken in by so many fraudulent promises, since there does not exist, on earth, any peace for men, even those, and especially those, of goodwill.

And why do I care about an *elsewhere*, which I could not imagine different enough from this *here*.

※

It is morning.

The bed, the feverish boat, is shipwrecked

Opening with a daybreak, this book ends with a daybreak.

The first was pierced with cold. Here, lying prone, is the last.

During the night, through the open window, came the moon and its evil spells. Insomnia drank the milky light, more poisonous than the milk of hemlock. And yet the same beverage was a filter for love affairs which thought they were eternal and peaceful, beneath the trees deep in the parks. So, many vanities can still come together. But you, who have my name and my face, just so many useless burdens, you're a shipwreck and won't accept help from anyone.

Immortal and glorious Hercules, you would have thrown yourself at the feet of Omphale.

A man as incapable of following an idea to its flaming limits as of expanding a defective thorax with full and rhythmical breathing after having in vain tried the appearance of innocence, this beautiful lost secret, you continue your solitary journey in the chaos of time. Your passage will be unmoving, like that of the coach whose wheels turned without moving whilst in the distance the fairy-tale scenes rushed by, dazzling you with a presentation of the life of Cinderella the first time you were taken to the theatre.

Like those scenes, mysterious *Gulf-streams* come, go, ploughing the waves of the spiritual map of the world where so many Americas remain to be discovered, of which Reason would wish to be a part but will not be Christopher Columbus.

Carried along by the currents, and not without hope of finding a harbour, for the most basic decency wants no further truck with the so-called God, the chairman of the boards of Eternity's insurance companies float about whilst waiting for death and its subterranean rivers, just float about.

And no sign of those ghostly vessels, religions, passing in the distance, at the horizon, not a cry in the direction of those hypothetical ships.

But, for those wandering from one bank to the other, for the cowards and the crooks who for social, jingoistic, conventional and other reasons, for the colourless admirers of multi-coloured lies, let your voice come back to life, billow and always and again ask:

Are you all crazy?

Are you all crazy?
If not...